Robert Edward Francillon

**Jack Doyle's Daughter**

Vol. 1

Robert Edward Francillon

**Jack Doyle's Daughter**
*Vol. 1*

ISBN/EAN: 9783337329518

Printed in Europe, USA, Canada, Australia, Japan

Cover: Foto ©Andreas Hilbeck / pixelio.de

More available books at **www.hansebooks.com**

BY

# R. E. FRANCILLON

AUTHOR OF ROPES OF SAND 'OLYMPIA 'A DOG AND HIS SHADOW' ETC.

IN THREE VOLUMES

## VOL. I.

London

# CHATTO & WINDUS, PICCADILLY

1894

PRINTED BY
SPOTTISWOODE AND CO., NEW-STREET SQUARE
LONDON

# CONTENTS

OF

# THE FIRST VOLUME

## PART I

### A DREADFUL DILEMMA

## PART II

### PHŒBE'S FATHERS

# PART III

## MISS DOYLE

# JACK DOYLE'S DAUGHTER

## PART I

### *A DREADFUL DILEMMA*

## CHAPTER I

### CHARLEY BASSETT AND HIS FOUR FRIENDS

It may be thought, by some fastidious people, that Mr. Charles Bassett, a young gentleman with a clear four hundred a year of his own, and first cousin to that eminent baronet, Sir Mordaunt Bassett, of Cautleigh Hall, Lincolnshire, had no business to be living in Bohemia at all. Even people holding more modern and less fastidious views of society may think it a little odd that an amateur Bohemian of his order, who could have made himself welcome and acceptable anywhere, should be hand-and-glove with such regular professional

Bohemians as Robert Urquhart, Richard Esdaile, Ulick Ronaine, and Jack Doyle—above all, with Jack Doyle.  But those times, though not very long ago, were not quite these.  Lords and ladies would as soon have thought of having a town house in Wapping, as of apeing the manners and customs of those who lived in Bohemia because they were obliged, and who, out of jovial defiance, sang the praises of what was but a land of more or less hard exile after all.  Think not you know our grim Siberian Bohemia of London, you who have in your heads pleasant dreams of the ghosts of Weimar, of the Caffè Greco, of the Latin Quarter!  It is not you who, with plenty of loose cash in your pockets, smoke in studios, get in the way of stage-carpenters, listen to the oracles of literary clubs, and can return among the Philistines whenever you please, who know what Bohemia means : you know it no more than he knows France who has travelled over every mile of every one of its railways. To-day, Charley Bassett as an amateur painter, musical composer, singer, pianist, dramatic author, critic, and poet, with a clear four hundred a year of his own, and of more than merely respectable connections, would have been a drawing-room lion ; he could have called himself 'Bohemian,' while living happily and comfortably in Philistia all the time. But the cant of his youth was of a rather different kind. The artist, instead of being a hero because he happens to earn his living by one sort of more or less honest work instead of another, was then hardly a respectable man ; and the gentleman who, out of natural eccentricity, preferred such society to that of his peers, required more than four hundred a year, and a better cousin than a baronet, in order to sit comfortably on both social stools. Now if Charley Bassett had a foible, it was a liking to lead without trouble, and to be accepted at his full value ; and if any man with four hundred a year and a baronet for a cousin doubts what these advantages will do for him in the Bohemia of fact and not of fancy, let him try ; he will not be long before he knows. For your true Bohemian is above all things human. Nay, his human nature is apt to take an exaggerated form. So Charley Bassett carried his talents, such as they were, into Bohemia, where he had been welcomed cordially.

So much for the amateur Bohemian, the sojourner in that never yet wholly explored and terribly misunderstood land. As for his friends, natives of the country, a few words will suffice for each of them.

Dick Esdaile, a plain young man with a whimsical twitch of the under lip, was—so his friends, who were not painters, held—the future Sir Richard Esdaile, P.R.A., who would make the whole world turn up its collective nose at the name of Michael Angelo. Meanwhile honest Dick smiled good-humouredly at the prophecy, and, while waiting for fame, worked as a deputy scene-painter at one of the theatres beyond Thames. He never spoke of his family, and was supposed to have fallen from the stars.

Ulick Ronaine was a Munster man, who, after studying, or otherwise, at half the medical schools of Ireland, Scotland, and Europe, had been attracted to London by a report he had heard of its being the biggest town in the world. For his ambitions, no less for his friends than for himself, were without bounds. He already had a good many patients, of a sort, for the simple reason that, though in all other matters as guileless as the day,

he practised an almost incredible amount
of foxlike cunning in evading the receipt
of fees. How, on such a system, he contrived to live at all, was a mystery that he
himself never attempted to unravel. He
did live, and that was all he knew or cared
to know.

Robert Urquhart was a philosopher from
Aberdeen, a student of the Middle Temple,
and a rigid economist, both political and social
—a character far more common in Bohemia
than is popularly supposed. He was the man
of theory and system, who reduced the commonest details of daily life to first principles,
and kept debtor-and-creditor accounts of
money and time. He considered neither as
wasted so long as it was properly set down,
balanced, and indexed. Esdaile had said of
him that he not only used to put down, under
the head ' Malt,' every glass of ale he drank,
but where, and when, and why, and of what
quality, and with what effect upon himself,
and at what cost, and at whose cost, and how
long, by the watch, it took in drinking, and
whether in combination with oysters, and if
so, with how many, together with the exact
latitude and longitude of the whole proceeding,

the direction and force of the wind, and the age of the moon.

But much as these three differed from one another, Jack Doyle, the big bearded man with the gruff growl and the ragged mane, differed yet more strongly from each and all. He was not more unlike Charley Bassett in his disreputable slovenliness of look and life than from Esdaile in his want of a career, from Ronaine in his want of reverence, and from Urquhart in a sublime ignorance of what the words 'law and order' mean. The others pinched or scrambled through life; he floundered and rolled—a notoriously, aggressively, typically penniless man, beyond the reach of aid. The only financially satisfactory thing about him was that he never borrowed—not even from such a Crœsus as Charley. When he had absolutely no money, he went without as long as nature could endure. When nature could no longer stand starvation, he went to bed and to sleep (men said that he never went to bed except on these occasions). When he could sleep no more, he knew how to find some sort of so-styled literary work, among the back slums of the press, whereby to put himself in funds again for a day or two. And

then he repeated the same course all over
again. Ronaine, who was no scholar, held
Jack Doyle to be the most learned man in
Europe ; but then, in Bohemia, every man
who does nothing is always credited with
being able to do everything if he pleased. He
was morose and sullen in bearing, even to a
point that looked like affectation; but was nevertheless not unsociable in his own way. He
would drop in upon men at the most unseason-
able and inconvenient hours, and would remain as long as he liked—which was generally for ever. Whence he had come into
Bohemia, nobody knew ; but he had become
so much part and parcel of it that men took
him as a matter of course, and never thought of
inquiring. He was never either drunk or
sober, and had rather less respect, if possible,
for women than he had for men. Perhaps
the day might come, not long hence, when
Bassett, Esdaile, Urquhart, and even Ronaine,
would learn to call Jack Doyle ' Blackguard.'
Meanwhile, they were young, and called him
' Friend,' with a youthful pride in his disreputable originality. None, as yet, could foresee
what growing old means in the case of a Jack
Doyle.

Charley Bassett lived in chambers at Number Forty-nine, Gray's Inn Square. His bedroom was up a good many stairs, but his sitting-room was rented of Messrs. Mark and Simple, solicitors, whose offices comprised the whole of the ground-floor. Bassett ' kept ' at the back, so that his window commanded a full and close view of the old terraced garden, where, among the black and learned-looking elms, and over the sombre turf, an ancient family of rooks, even in the heart of London, still build and caw. The quietest of bachelor students could ask for no better home. Around and above was heard, by day, nothing noisier than the occasional smothered slam of a baize door, or the caw of the rooks, which never jars the most finely-strung nerves ; by night not even the hum of Holborn, though so near, could find its way in.

There was a good deal of character about Charley Bassett's room. Elegant bachelorhood had not yet become an everyday thing, especially in the least fashionable of the Inns of Court, so that Charley must have been not a little in advance of his time. The room was studio, boudoir, library, and smoking-room in one. The furniture was arranged with a view to effect which, though it would have given any modern æsthete a fit of the horrors, was meant to be artistic in a humble and benighted way. A few tolerable oil paintings were on the walls ; an easel, with a splashed canvas, stood in one corner, and a cottage piano in another, while books, for the most part gorgeously bound, filled a whole wall. There were even flowers, whose breath served to call special attention to a more general aroma of turpentine, Russia leather, and ghosts of cigars whose name must have been legion, and of that indefinable essence which, when it comes through an open window on a warm evening, tells a blind man that he is in London, and nowhere else in the world.

Charley Bassett himself sat alone at that open window, taking things very easily indeed. The summer evening was young, but yet, one would think, too old for slippers and dressing-gown and for the fresh remains, on a corner table, of a meal that looked suspiciously like breakfast. Slippers, dressing-gown, and embroidered smoking-cap were each and all of a pattern much harder to describe than that of their wearer. He was a consciously hand-

some young man of five-and-twenty at most,
lazy and languid in his poses, but looking
very well able to look quite otherwise if the
humour should seize him; healthily pale in
complexion, with grey eyes, and almost
femininely delicate lips full of good humour
and good nature, with a firmly-marked nose
and chin, and thick clustering brown hair.
To match the splendour of his costume, he
had adopted the then purely artistic affectation of a moustache, cheeks and chin being
clean shaved.

Whatever were his reflections, he was
evidently not a man who knew much about
unhappy ones. Clearly, if he was in love, he
had been accepted; if he had accepted any
bills, they were obviously not nearly due.
Nor, on the other hand, were they so all-
absorbing as to make solitude a necessity.
Not a shadow of a frown crossed his forehead when the thump of a heavy fist fell upon
the outer door, and was followed by an
imitation of a solo on the big drum. On the
contrary, he rose and opened to the performers with unmistakably hearty welcome.
'Come in, you fellows. You've strangled an
epic in the bud, as Ronaine would say, but

never mind. I've got plenty more growing. What do you want? Breakfast? I've had my own—but then, you know, I'm an uncommonly early bird.'

Charley's friends were as unlike as no doubt Pylades and Orestes were, and, at the same time, no less unlike Charley. One was a very dark, sallow-complexioned lad, apparently made entirely of exceedingly tough wire, with high cheek bones, deep eyes, an aquiline nose, and a hard and hungry expression which gave him the look of a famished bird of prey. He, was dressed neatly and quietly, and bore no sign about him of sharing Charley's artistic fopperies. Short of inches as well as of flesh, he did not reach the shoulders of his companion, who had the self-consciously tall man's trick of stooping as he came through the door. Not only was the latter full six feet high, but was of a breadth and girth that required all his inches to carry fairly. If his friend was a hungry hawk, he was a dissipated lion. There was leonine flatness as well as breadth about so much of his face as was unhidden by a full tawny beard, while the mane was well represented by a heavy mass of tangled chestnut

hair, touched on the temples with grey—the
results of that form of Time which is to be
measured by nights instead of days.  For
there was an air of general bedlessness about
him ; his complexion was puffed and blotched,
his eyes heavy and bleared, his hands unclean,
his linen soiled and crumpled, and his badly-
made clothes tumbled on anyhow.

'Breakfast?' growled the latter, deeply,
gruffly, and slowly.  'Yes, I've heard of
breakfast, it's something they give you for
dinner in farmhouses, I believe ; or where is
it they give it to you?  Yes, I'll take one.
One ought to try everything once.  If I don't
like it, I needn't do it again.'

'Vera well put, Jack Doyle,' said his
younger companion in a dry tone of didactic
approval.  'Vera well put, indeed.  Experience, which is but the soom total of separate
experiments, is just the entire basis of philosophy.  Ye may think half-past six o'clock
is a bit late for breakfast.  So it may be.
But then so, ye see, it may not be.  Nobody
can tell the best time for breakfast till he's
fairly tried every minute of the one thousand
four hundred and forty that go to a day.  As
ye vera justly say, a man must try everything

before he knows anything, for till he knows everything he knows nothing—nothing at all.'

'Then, on that showing,' said Charley, bringing out decanters and glasses, 'you must commit at least one murder before you can claim to be the infinitesimal fraction of a philosopher? By Jove, Urquhart, when I defend you at the Old Bailey for murdering your great-grandmother, I shall go in for an acquittal on the ground of experimental philosophy.'

'My great-grandmother?' exclaimed Urquhart, a little quickly. 'Why, she died sixty years ago—before I was born! And if she were living—if ye think I'll evacuate a philosophical position from any fear of the consequences it leads to—then ye know vera little of me ; vera little indeed.'

'But how about suicide, eh?' asked Charley. 'Mustn't you try that, too? And about drinking bad port? or about——'

'Ye can't tell if the port is bad,' said Urquhart, 'till ye've tried. And as to suicide——'

'All port's good,' growled Doyle, 'when you can't get brandy. And as to suicide—

when you can't do better, that's good too.
But, as I see breakfast's nothing but Latin for
brandy, I can do better than port or poison
for to-night, or to-day, or to-morrow, or
yesterday, or whatever it is ; and since I can,
I will. That's my philosophy, Urquhart. So
here goes.'

'On the contrary,' remonstrated Urquhart,
'it is not philosophy at all. It is not even
theory. Why, it would be just laughed at
in Aberdeen.'

'Never mind, old fellow,' said Charley.
'Leave Jack there alone. Practice first,
theory after—your own doctrine, you know.
You're all right both of you. "Leap before
you look"—that's the finest maxim old Bacon
ever made. Come—shut up. I know everything you're going to say about Mary Queen
of Scots before you begin. By Jove, talking
of Mary Queen of Scots, there's a deuced
pretty girl just where I saw the ghost of Lord
Bacon—he hung out in this Inn, you know—
five minutes ago. Isn't she, Jack Doyle ?
Bring your tumbler to the window, and see
if the black old garden doesn't look a shade
and a half brighter than it did half a minute
ago. Holloa ! Get out all the tumblers you

can find in the cupboard, Jack—I'm in for a
levée, it seems.'

So it did seem, to judge from new thunder
on the outer door. Again Charley opened;
but again to no more than two visitors, in
spite of a preliminary battery that had promised at least a score.

The new-comers were hailed as 'Esdaile'
and 'Ronaine.' Esdaile was a short, stout-
built, sturdy young fellow, so commonplace
in feature that it is needless to consider
whether he was pale or red, dark or fair.
His small insignificant eyes were quick and
clear, and a slight chronic twitch about the
corners of his mouth betrayed an inveterate
habit of silent jesting. Ronaine's features, on
the other hand, were, happily, not common
at all. A rough, formless face, looking for
all the world as if it belonged to an india-
rubber toy in one of its most grotesque contortions; a flattened up-turned nose, and a
cloven and twisted chin, a freckled complexion, thick lips that never touched one
another, a low knotted brow, a pair of light
blue eyes thrown in anyhow, a thin crop of
straight sandy hair, a lank figure to match
the face—thus would Ronaine be represented

by the sun of the photographers, who re-
produces so faithfully everything about a man
except that which is alone worth reproducing.
What on earth does it signify whether a nose
turns up or down? For about Ronaine's
ugliness, young though he was, there was
something positively winning, he carried it so
simply and so bravely. No true friend of
Ronaine's would have wished him less unlike
Adonis by the breadth of a hair.

The atmosphere of the room rose per-
ceptibly as he came in; even sullen and dull
Jack Doyle nodded to him with a quarter of
a smile.

'Well, you fellows,' said Ronaine, with a
pleasant dash of rough brogue, and the most
hideously genial of smiles, 'an' what mischief
are y'up to now? There's a regular triangle
of ye. But ye'll have to find two more
corners in it for me and Esdaile, if there's any
sort of fun alive.'

'Any amount of room here for anybody
who wants anything, as long as he's content
to want nothing but what he finds,' said
Charley, throwing rather more than half a
cigar through the open window—for he held
it an insult to a fine cigar to worry it after its

first freshness had gone. 'We're looking at a pretty girl in the garden. Come to the front, Ronaine. Contrast is Art's first law.'

'Faith, Charley, I will. All the beauty shan't be on the other side. . . . So, that's what ye call a pretty girl, is it, in London? I suppose ye'll be calling Venus a pretty girl next, and be hanged to ye. In Ireland we call things by their right names, and when we see a real angel of loveliness like that, we say so—and to her face too! And I've half a mind I will.'

'I'd like to see that experiment,' said Urquhart. 'There's no knowing how a girl will take anything till ye've tried.'

'H'm!' muttered Esdaile dryly. 'I suppose what Charley Bassett would say to any common duchess will be quite good enough for Jack Doyle to say to a slightly less ordinary nursemaid, or housemaid, or whatever Ronaine's last new Venus may chance to be. Why don't you look out at window, Jack? For she is a pretty girl —as girls go, in these degenerate days.'

'Why don't I? Because I've seen pretty girls before, and don't admire the breed,' growled Jack Doyle from his tumbler. 'Well, boys ; you're all young yet. Look away if you like, but don't bother me till you've done. I hate petticoats. They do nothing but upset the drink, and set good fellows by the ears.'

# CHAPTER II

## AN UNBIDDEN GUEST

'WELL,' said Jack, stretching himself after half a doze, and draining his tumbler, 'isn't she gone?'

'To tell you the truth,' said Charley, 'she isn't yet fairly in view. We're in the position of a lot of astronomers waiting for the transit of Venus. At present she's only a telescopic star, pacing yon distant terrace like a sentry on duty.'

'Or waiting for one off duty,' interrupted Esdaile. 'Where a red-coat's concerned, it's always she that waits for him—never he for her. That's a fine poetical image, though, about a telescopic star walking up and down like full-private Atkins. Ronaine couldn't beat that, Charley, in his best brogue.'

'"And sentinel stars set their watch in the sky,"' sang Bassett. 'But, look out. Here she comes! Here she—— Oh, hang it all;

c 2

she is a nursemaid, after all! A young woman, with a —— baby. You called her Venus, just now, doctor. You're only too right—there's Cupid too.'

'Venus be hanged in her own zone,' said Doyle. 'I came here to be amused. I've got to write my sermon to-night.'

'What? By Jove, Jack, if I didn't suspect you, from the first moment I set eyes on you, of being an archdeacon in disguise—particularly in disguise! I should like to hear a sermon of yours, Jack, I must say.'

'Go to church next Sunday, then,' said Jack, 'if you know the way there. And the betting's five thousand to one you'll hear me.'

'Only name the church, and I'm there,' said Charley. 'If I don't know the way myself, I can find a cabman that will.'

'There are ten thousand parishes in England. Do you think there are ten thousand Englishmen who can write fifty-two sermons a year? Do you think there are a hundred Englishmen who can write one real sermon in fifty years? I tell you, writing a sermon is a tougher job than adapting a farce, any day. Parsons are public-school boys, nine out of ten; so they can't often so much as spell. But

most of them have got an odd half-crown, so
we swap silver and brains. Tall church, short
church, thick church, thin church—I've got
to be pretty well up in the slang of them all.
But it's a matter of three-and-sixpence to-night,
so I've got to turn on the agony tap specially
strong. I want an idea, well filtered through
the commonest brains I can find. Give me
one. Is she tall or short, thick or thin?'

'I do not vera clearly perceive,' said
Urquhart, ' the association of ideas between a
sermon and a——'

'Petticoat?' growled Doyle. 'Turn
curate yourself, my lad; and you'll know all
about it in half an hour.'

'Jack's in thorough bad form to-night,'
said Bassett aside to Ronaine, as the two
leaned together half out of the window with
their elbows on the sill. 'I shall have to
choose between giving him in charge of the
nearest cabman, and keeping him till he walks
home. I don't pretend to go in for piety
myself, but, hang it all, don't you know, one
must draw the line somewhere.'

'Is it bad form?' said the doctor out loud.
'Faith, if it's bad form not to look at an angel
of loveliness when he's got the chance, then

Jack Doyle's up to his scalp, and that's over most men's, in bad form. He doesn't deserve to be told what he's losin'.'

'And he isn't ass enough,' said Doyle, 'to want anything he deserves. He wants what he does not deserve. He wants ambrosia, and nectar, and the root of the lotus, and a tankard of Lethe, neat, to wash it all down. Come, shepherd swains of Gray his Inn—Tune up your pipes, and eke begin—To praise yon nymph, that so ye may—My long ears tickle with your bray.'

Charley Bassett was not the man to play second fiddle when the gauntlet of rhyme was thrown down before him.

'Tall, fair, and slim is she, I ween—Who treads alone yon garden green—Scares Learning's ghosts with Beauty's charms—And . . . And . . . H'm . . . And . . .'

'And holds an Infant in her arms,' said Esdaile. 'By Jove, when you go in for laureate, Charley, you'll have to run me hard.'

'If ye like to call five feet two inches tall,' objected Urquhart, 'then she is tall. I've got as good an eye for height as any man going.'

'Five feet two!' said Bassett scornfully. 'Five feet two and a half at least, if she's one. I'm not going to have anybody's poetry spoiled by any man's prose. "Short, fair, and slim " — what a line ! Beats even Esdaile's——'

'Poetry,' said Urquhart dogmatically, ' is just senseless and freevolous rubbish if it does not express truth better than common prose can. But to do that, it must express truth at least as well as prose. And accuracy is the very first condition of truth ; and I'll not let myself be contradicted there. I tell ye that a poem that just expresses the plain, simple, downright truth about anything is better than the finest of any other kind.'

'There can, of course, be no question,' said Bassett, ' that " Thirty days hath September " is the finest poem in the world. Not even Shakespeare ever wrote anything like that. Nobody's going to contradict you, Urquhart ; but what then ?'

' Why, that " tall " and " short " are just comparative terms, that mean just nothing at all. And so I say——'

' I suppose this is your notion of a love poem, Urquhart :

The maid for whom I sigh alack,
IIas eyes of blue and boots of black,
In which she stands, July eleventh,
Five feet, five inches, and a seventh.'

'If ye make it two inches,' said Urquhart, 'I'll say it's better poetry, because it's better truth than I've heard for a long time. If ye think I'm going to surrender a philosophical position from fear of the consequences, or of freevolous hypercriticism, then ye know vera little of me—vera little indeed.'

'And it's blue, ye call that girl's eyes?' broke in Ronaine. 'Faith, they may be called blue in England, but they're what we call black in Ireland—as black and as bright as a pair of blazing coals——'

'Put it into verse, doctor,' said Bassett, 'or you'll be fined all round. Or I'll bet you even money they're blue, and you'll lose. Now look here, Jack Doyle, as you've made yourself umpire, I'll give you her description like a policeman. Apparent age, nineteen; height——'

'Nineteen? Five-and-twenty, more likely,' said Urquhart. 'Look at her figure——'

'Don't interrupt the court,' said Bassett. 'Age, nineteen; height, five feet five; figure——'

'Two,' said Urquhart. 'Two and a quarter, at the outside.'

'You're fined for contempt. Five feet five; figure, slender; eyes, blue——'

'Black, ye mane,' burst in Ronaine. 'Faith, I never heard black eyes called blue in my life before.'

'Complexion, rosy; nose, retroussé; hair, darkish brown; air, pensive; calling, unknown; dress——'

'Divil take the rags!' said Ronaine. 'Will we talk about a girl as if she'd be a horse, if ye plase? She's the loveliest brunette, Jack Doyle, ye ever set eyes on: with cheeks like peaches and eyes like sloes, and as tall as a lily and as full as a rose. As like an angel, Jack, as ye ever saw——'

'Jack Doyle being so particularly in the habit of entertaining angels,' said Esdaile. 'By Jove, the doctor's turned out the laureate after all. But she isn't a bad-looking young woman, all the same, if you add Bassett's passport to the doctor's idyll and divide by two. Her cheeks are not quite like peaches, and I shouldn't admire them if they were;

but they're good articles of their kind ; and
her eyes which are grey, by the way, are all
the better for being more useful to see with
than a couple of vegetables would be.  As to
lilies and roses, I suppose that's poetry for
anything you please ; and as to height, well,
say five four—a good useful height for a
strapping nursemaid.   And as to the rest—
not above chaff, I should say.   Our good
company doesn't seem to keep her from
coming this way.   There she is for you, Jack,
sketched on a thumb-nail.'

'I'll settle that question,' said Jack Doyle
suddenly.   He rose, lounged heavily to
the window, reached out more than half
his bulk, and shouted, in a thunderous
voice :

'I say, young woman, how tall are you?
And without your boots, mind !'

'Hullo, Jack !' cried Charley, 'I say, that
won't do.   That isn't the way to do things
at all.'

He, also, leaned out of window, and
declaimed, out of an unperformed extrava-
ganza of his own writing :

'Vouchsafe, illustrious damsel, to expound
How far thine orbs transcend terrestrial ground ?

Now, Urquhart, a guinea to eighteenpence, she's five feet five.'

The girl, who had been straying towards the window, not wholly unconscious of being looked at, looked up suddenly at Jack Doyle's summons; then, seeing Charley's handsome face and magnificence of costume, let her eyes meet his for an instant, by no means angrily; and then looked up at the rooks' nests on the tops of the trees. Two things that had been said of her were unmistakably true—she was a pretty girl, and was carrying a baby. As to the rest, who shall decide when Charley Bassett and his friends—each, save perhaps Jack Doyle, a doctor in such matters—had hopelessly disagreed?

Charley had caught the glance—he had caught many such in his time—and smiled.

'I pause for a reply,' said he. 'Never mind the big fellow; he shan't eat you. Look after that baby, that's all.'

'Yes, he looks like that,' she said, with a toss of her head that was certainly not meant to be thrown away upon unappreciative eyes.

'Looks like what?' said Charley.

'Never you mind. But baby shan't hurt him. He needn't be afraid. I'll take care.'

'One for you, Jack!' said Charley. 'You'd better put yourself inside again.'

'No, my dear, it isn't the baby we're afraid of—it's you. You're a most dangerous young person, and I shall speak to the porter not to let you in again. You are not only interrupting our studies, but you have been making us all quarrel about you as we never quarrelled about anything before. I shall have a special bencher set in the garden to keep out every girl who is prettier than she ought to be.'

'As if there wasn't some faces at that very window that's fit to scare off anybody you want to! I noticed how the gardens weren't very full, and it couldn't have been the porter kept people out; he was good-looking enough, and he had a civil tongue besides.'

'One for you, Ronaine, this time!' said Charley. 'So take the thing you call your face in. It's your turn now, Urquhart. You've got experience to go upon now, you know. Allow me, my dear, to introduce you to a friend who was never put down in an argument yet, and never will be. My friend, Professor Mac Plato—Miss, miss, miss—if I

haven't forgotten your name already!
Miss——'

'Seeing you never knew it, forgetting's no
wonder. And what's more, you won't get it
by asking out of me.'

'Fool that I was, not to see that you
are the Marchioness of Clerkenwell in
disguise! But your ladyship need fear
nothing from me : your secret is as safe as
if it were my own. I assure your ladyship
that your ladyship need not be in the least
afraid.'

'As if—if I wanted to be afraid,' said
the girl, tossing her head again. 'I'd
begin with you. I can give as good as
I get ; so don't you make any mistake
there !'

'Come, Charley,' said Esdaile, ' we've had
enough of this for to-day. I can't say that
the brilliancy of the wit is quite up to the
mark on either side. Blow her a kiss, and
when she doesn't see your head-dress any
more at the window, perhaps she'll move
on.'

'Ah, you're jealous, I see, because you
don't know how to talk to a marchioness
and because I do. Perhaps you're right

about the wit, but you can't have everything.
The girl is pretty; and not bad fun either,
to my mind. Don't you like the way she
poses herself to be looked at, and waits
to be talked to, and carries indignant modesty
to every point short of—moving on? I called
her a marchioness because I've seen the same
thing among that sort of people hundreds of
times; only they don't do it in Belgravia
half so honestly. Look how slowly she
begins to creep off, an inch an hour, and
works her shoulders as she goes; the least
grain of chaff, good or bad, would bring
her to again. Marchioness or milkmaid,
I'd undertake to whistle her through the
window in an hour. I do like a bit of
human nature, Dick, and it's there. Call it
vulgar if you like, but it's there. I'm
engaged in one of Urquhart's experiments,
you see.'

'And the more shame for you, Charley,'
said Ronaine. 'There's nothing bad about
the girl, that I can see, and if there was,
trate her as if there wasn't, and lave her
alone.'

'That's just what she doesn't want to
be left,' said Bassett, 'and what woman wills,

you know—— But I do not make a mistake,'
he called from the window. 'I assure you
I am incapable of such a thing. You are
afraid! you are running away this very
minute, as if you had a whole troop of
the Blues at your heels—you know you
are.'

Bassett was right; the girl turned round
and smiled without any pretence of anger.
'That's how much I'm afraid,' said she.
'Perhaps I might be afraid of the Blues; but
the Blues wouldn't sit safe at their windows
and take precious good care not to come down
—not they!'

'I confess I am incapable of matching
your ladyship in knowledge of the manners
and customs of the Life Guards Blue. Ah!
it's all very well not to be afraid of five
poor old bookworms like us, who dare not
come into the open air for fear of catching
our deaths of cold. But you know you
wouldn't dare trust yourself on our side
of the window. Yes, I most decidedly
advise you to stay outside. We are lambs
out of doors, but we're terrible fellows
at home. Talk of the Blues, indeed?
Did you ever hear of Bluebeard? We're he.'

'Ah, I s'pose you think I'm one of them that's caught by curiosity,' said the girl. 'I know a trick worth two of that.'

'Fine talking! You know all the time you wouldn't go through that archway, and into Number Forty-nine in the Square, even for the sake of showing you're not afraid of me.'

'Wouldn't I though! But I'm not going to, because I won't; so you needn't try to play your tricks. This is the baby, not me.'

'So I see; and though you pretend to be so brave, you wouldn't even trust your baby here, for fear he—she—it—should never come out again alive.'

'And no more it would,' said the girl. 'Why, you'd be holding it all legs upwards, poor little dear, and dropping it in the fender, and I don't know what and all—and a nice hot scolding I should have for supper when I got home. Trust you with a baby indeed! —not I.'

'On the contrary; if there is one thing I have studied more closely and exhaustively than another, it is the art of nursing. Indeed, I myself have been a baby, so I

have had special and personal opportunities——'

'Not you. I don't believe you've
ever——'

'Been a baby? But I have, indeed. As
you seem, however, to doubt my skill, hand
it up and see.'

'Why, you'd drop it half-way.'

'I wouldn't drop it a quarter of the way.
Come, a child ought to see a little of life, you
know. And one ought to do everything once,
as a friend of mine here present tells me. If
I don't like it, I needn't do it again. Come,
who's afraid now? I'll lay you a new bonnet
to nothing that I hold that specimen of
humanity, that undeveloped microcosm, as
well as if I were the great-grandfather of ten.
There's a fair offer of a new bonnet, and I'm
a man of my word.'

'Faith, and I'd like myself to see Charley
with a baby!' chuckled Ronaine, who really
had some professional knowledge of the topic.
'Wouldn't you, now, Archdeacon Jack?'

But Jack Doyle was in the land of dreams.

'Two to one, Urquhart,' said Esdaile, 'he
takes hold by one leg instead of two. In
half-crowns. Done?'

'It may be more interesting than ye think,' said Urquhart. 'It is of very grave scientific consequence to observe how a mon, with only the inner consciousness to guide him, will act under circumstances that are entirely new to that mon. It will be an important experiment in relation to the doctrine of innate and original ideas, which I wholly repudiate, as ye know. So up with the bairn, my lass.'

'Carried,' said Bassett, 'nem. con. Now then, my dear, prove you're the bravest girl out by trusting a man with a baby.'

'I'd as soon trust one with my Sunday bonnet. You'll drop it on the gravel, as sure as you're there.'

'How can you tell till I've tried? Besides, we keep a surgeon on the premises, and if it's quite smashed I'll buy you another, as good as new. Come, that bonnet to a lock of your hair I give it you back safe and sound.'

'As if I'd give my hair to the likes of you! But there, I do like to see the conceitedness of the men. They all think they can do everything till they try. There; try away!'

Charley Bassett reached out, took the child from the lifted arms of the girl, did not drop it, and set it up, awkwardly enough, on the sill of the window. It was a very small creature of scarcely more than a year old, but healthy-looking, and, on opening its dark eyes, it set up a crow instead of a cry in honour of its new situation.

'What the deuce is that?' suddenly growled Jack Doyle, whose eyes opened simultaneously with the baby's.

'It is dangerous, by Jove!' laughed Charley, as the creature made a claw at the doctor's face, and crowed again. 'Here, take it yourself, Jack; I'm hanged if I do know how to hold the thing after all; or you, doctor, it's more in your line than the parson's. Hollo, young woman! What are you hanging about outside my window for, if you please?'

'I'll thank you for the child again, now you've found out how holding one's none so easy. Next time you'll be less free with your bonnets, may be.'

'Child? bonnet? Excuse me, my good girl, but I don't know what you mean. This is not a milliner's, and I assure you Messieurs Mark and Simple would be aghast at the very idea of an infant, not in Chancery, at Number

Forty-nine, Gray's Inn Square. We are young men whose prospects in life depend upon our characters. Go away.'

'Ah, that's what's called chaff, I suppose. But it'll be no fun to me when I catch it for not being home by supper-time.'

'Catch it then; one, two, three, and away!' said Ronaine, making a pretence of throwing the baby through the window pantomime-fashion. But Bassett stopped his arm.

'I forbid infanticide in my chambers,' said he. 'My dear girl, there is a child here, and in the direst peril. Here's a dignitary of the Church who wants to drown it in brandy, and a doctor wants to throw it out of the window, and a painter who wants to take its likeness, and a philosopher who wants to cut it open to see what's inside, and how it's made. I, who would protect it, am but one to four. Would you save it from four terrible dooms, there's but one thing for it. You must come round yourself and fetch it away.'

'No nonsense for me!' said the girl sharply, holding up her arms. But it was with a glance at Bassett which seemed to contradict the sharpness of her tone.

Flirtation with a stray nursemaid might not be held a high form of sport even in his set, where tastes in such matters had to adapt themselves to their opportunities. But the girl was really pretty, and Charley liked to be glanced at in that way.

'Nonsense?' he asked; 'I wouldn't presume—and it's not nonsense at all. If you want to see this child again, here you must come. Number Forty-nine in the Square, through the archway. Mark and Simple in whitish letters on the door—ground-floor. I have sworn it, and never did I break an oath to a woman, so long as I meant to keep it, since I was born. Far less would I dream of breaking one made to you. There.' He slammed the window down and drew the blind. 'There,' said he. 'I said I could make her come in a minute if I chose. Act Two, Scene One—enter the Marchioness of Clerkenwell, seeking her child.'

'And exit too, I hope,' said Esdaile. 'I've had enough of this game.'

'Poor, miserable little imp!' said Jack Doyle. 'To think of our having been once like that——'

'Speak for your venerable self, arch-

deacon,' said Bassett. 'I never sat among a
company of scamps, drinking, and chaffing
innocent young women, before I was two
years old. Well, my little chap, and what do
you think of us all—eh? I'll bet you a rattle
you never had such an experience as this
since you were born. Pass the little chap the
'baccy, Urquhart, and a clean clay, and the
bottle, and we'll let him see what making a
night of it means before he goes home. Make
your head while you're young, as Bacon
says somewhere. Hollo, doctor! what the
deuce is it up to now? What is it going to
do?'

'Pooh! Only going to sleep,' said
Ronaine. 'Chuck it on to the sofa—no: the
other way up, if you don't want to study
apoplexy. That'll do. Hark! there's the
nurse at the door.'

Bassett opened and looked out.

'No,' said he. 'Nothing but one of the
ghosts out of the hall. She'll have to be fined
for keeping the stage waiting. And, in all
solemn honesty, I wish she would come, for
I've had enough of this nonsense myself by
now.'

'I suppose she's punishing us a bit—and

serve us right too,' said Esdaile. 'It is nonsense. What made you go in for it, Charley?
I'm hanged if I know.'

'Do you suppose I know it myself?' asked
Charley. 'Urquhart's the only man I ever
heard of who knows why he does things.
There's one thing I do like about women.
They're never afraid to own that they do
things because they do.'

'And what'll ye do with the girl when she
comes?' asked Urquhart gravely. 'If ye
want her, vera well; but if ye don't, ye'll find
her, may be, harder to get out than to get in.'

'True, O philosopher! And therefore I
shall not let her in. I shall give her the brat
at the door, and dismiss her like a father, with
a kiss and a blessing. Or we'll toss for a kiss,
for anything I care. What shall we do to
begin with—nothing or something? Improv-
ing conversation, or loo?'

'Loo,' said Jack Doyle. 'If I lose, I'll
make my sermon against gambling. If I win,
I shall be saved from having to write one at
all.'

'Loo, by all means,' said Esdaile. 'I want
to make a few millions. Wasn't that a tap,
Charley? I'll go and see while you're shuffling

the cards. No. This ought to be the first of April, it seems to me.'

Bassett set out a card-table, and the game began. It must not be for a moment supposed that these men played according to the measure of their means. On the contrary, the Russian prince of fiction who trusts a whole province to the hazard of a die, would have called this high play. Thousands and tens of thousands were the lowest stakes heard of after the first ten minutes of the game, and the interests of the players became as great as if the colossal fortunes at stake existed anywhere but in their own combined imaginations. There would have been no excitement at all in playing for anything that their combined purses could pay. Bassett, indeed, kept perfectly cool, being really well enough off to take such child's play at its proper value. But Urquhart looked as sharply after every bone counter as if it were one of those famous sixpences by which his beautifully-balanced finances were mostly measured. Esdaile became earnest. Ronaine threw away his hereditary acres, and their millions of rent, with the furious recklessness only to be matched by the fever with which Jack Doyle

gathered them in. The latter spoke no word
beyond an occasional triumphant exclamation
when he made some coup. If Fortune was
his foe, her phantom was marvellously his
friend.

'Nine!'

It was the bell of Charley Bassett's clock
that spoke. And at the same moment
another slighter but far more alarming sound
happened to catch Ronaine's ear.

'Murder an' blazes!' cried he. 'It
wasn't seven, Charley, when ye slammed the
window; and now 'tis nine, and 'tis there
still!'

'What's there?' asked Charley, looking
up from his deal. 'The window?'

'No, the child!'

'By Jove!' The cards fell from Charley's
startled hand.

'Come, don't break a run of luck like
this,' thundered Doyle. 'Go on, Charley, go
on. I mean to win five millions before I've
done. Play!'

But nobody heeded him. All eyes were
turned upon the sofa in a fixed gaze of would-
be comic despair.

'This is simply awful!' said Charley at last. 'My friends, I blush to confess it—but—we're sold!'

'In all my experience——' began Urquhart.

'No, Charley!' broke in Ronaine. 'I'll not believe that of nurse or mother. 'Tis against nature that a woman would leave a child——'

'H'm!' said Esdaile. 'Maternal instinct may be a very pretty thing in poetry, but it doesn't keep little girls from breaking their dolls or big ones from dropping theirs into the Thames, or leaving them at stray doors. I've known them get rid of encumbrances in worse ways. Charley's right, Ronaine. A joke wouldn't have lasted two mortal hours.'

'A joke, indeed!' said Charley. 'Three several times I told her where to come, and how to get here. She'd have been here in a quarter of a minute; and a joke of that sort, with a girl like that, would have lasted half a quarter of an hour. No, she wanted to be rid of that child, and we were fools enough to show her how it might be done.'

'Are you a king or an editor, Charley, that you say " We " for " I " ? ' said Esdaile.

'But never mind that. I won't be hard on a man when he's down.'

'Perhaps, then,' said Charley, for the first time showing signs of temper, 'your wisdom will be able to tell my folly what's to be done.'

Uneasy silence fell like a cloud—of tobacco smoke, for it took that form—over the whole company. Not even Ronaine could find a laugh, in the face of such an awful situation. The terrible baby slept calmly on.

Suddenly Jack Doyle rubbed his eyes, and let his millions melt away into their native air. 'Do you mean to say,' he asked, 'that we've —got—that—child—on—our—hands ?'

'Aye, archdeacon. Bring your mind to earth; for the question is how to get what we've got on our hands off again.'

Jack half staggered from his chair, lurched over to the sofa, and looked down, for the space of a full minute, upon his sleeping fellow-creature.

'Wring its neck!' said he, and lurched back to his chair.

'As a last resource,' began Charley thoughtfully. 'But, before we have to adopt such extreme measures—wait a bit.'

He went to the door, and shouted with the full force of his lungs :

'Admiral Horatio Collingwood Nelson, ahoy !'

# CHAPTER III

## PATRES CONSCRIPTI

HE who answered the summons was probably,
on an average, a man of about thirty-four
years old—on an average, because thirty-
four, which he certainly was not, is the mean
between eighteen and fifty. His age might
be either of the two extremes. Possibly he
was really thirty-four, and that one-half of
him had prematurely hurried on to fifty
while the other half had been content to stand
still at eighteen. Admiral Horatio Collingwood Nelson was weedy looking, with sloping
shoulders and a long weak neck, like a boy
who has outgrown his strength—an effect
that was further carried out by a perfectly
smooth, unwrinkled face, and by the manner
in which his wrists and ankles projected from
their proper coverings. He had an inky look,
moreover, as if he had just been up to his ears
in an exercise that obliged his pen to search for

inspiration among the roots of his hair. But then, on the other hand, that same hair was extant only in the form of a pinkish-grey fringe round a scalp that shone like a polished mirror ; and the careworn, anxious, down-beaten expression of his face could never have been achieved by a boy. His features were all exaggerated, without being remarkable. The chin was too short, the forehead too smooth and high, the nose too long and fleshy, the eyes too weakly and mildly blue. The mouth, through all his general air of being overladen with anxiety, smiled meekly and softly, almost like a very aged child's. There was not much of the naval officer about the cut of his clothes—a very old dress-coat, well greased and very grey at the seams, and buttoned across the chest wherever a button remained ; a pink-and-white shirt collar, tied with a large white methodist bow ; shapeless grey trousers, with a broad stripe down the outer sides ; a pair of low shoes, tied with ribbons. Behind one large crimson ear he carried a quill pen, and held a long ruler in one of his bony and elaborately white hands.

'Admiral,' said Charley, 'go into the archway, and if you find the murdered corpse of a young woman, just let me know.'

'Yes, Mr. Bassett,' said the admiral, with a feeble and flickering smile. 'Is there anything else I can do for you, by the way?'

'Ah! there spoke the British sailor. No questions, no surprise, all eagerness to do more than his duty. Yes. If you find no corpse, go round the Square and see if there's any young woman anywhere about looking for a baby. If there is, bring her here.'

'Yes, Mr. Bassett, certainly. I'll see. If I find a baby looking about the Square after a murdered corpse, I'm to bring them here. Yes, Mr. Bassett, it shall be done.'

'No, admiral—a live girl, looking for a live baby. Here, drink that, and be-gone.'

'That's a mighty queer admiral, en-tirely!' said Ronaine, as soon as the messenger had gulped down the contents of a tumbler and had set off on his errand. 'Who'll he be?'

'Horatio Collingwood Nelson! That's

his name.   And I believe he makes incredible
efforts to live up to the responsibilities his
godfathers and godmothers thought fit to lay
on him.   A sort of copying-clerk, or odd-job
man—a " super," in fact, to Mark and Simple ;
but with a soul above his station, you see ; a
lion in a lamb's skin, or a lamb in a lion's—I
hardly know which to say.   Mark my words :
if there ever be a republic in England,
Horatio Collingwood Nelson will be its first
president, as sure as that confounded baby's
on that sofa.   He's the most thorough-
going desperado—deep down—that I ever
knew : a cross between a British pirate and
a French regicide, Captain Kidd and Marat
rolled into one.   He'll be heard of one of
these days.'

'You take things easy, Charley,' said
Esdaile, ' I must say.   That child——'

'Won't be got rid of by taking things
hard.   We must first know if the girl's
really and truly gone.   If I do seem to take
things easy——'

'He's bock!' exclaimed Urquhart, who
had never taken his eyes from the clock
since the messenger had left the room.

'Well, admiral,' asked Bassett, betraying,

by the very lightness of his tone, more Philistine anxiety than he cared to show, 'dead or
alive?'

But the admiral's manner was strangely
changed. The lion seemed to have thrown
off his lamb's wool.

'And I must and I do say, Mr. Bassett,' he
began, in shrill oratorical style, 'that it is not
from you, nor from gentlemen that are
gentlemen, being friends of yours, which I
looked to be treated in a way which I can
only term as un-English, Mr. Bassett, sir; and
I furthermore and moreover do say that to
despatch an individual, whosoever he may be,
to search after corpses and such-like articles
in squares and arches, when there's nothing
of the species on the premises, is not consi-
derate of the comfort or dignity of that individual. If it was the first of April, Mr.
Bassett, I could make allowance for the high
spirits of youth in the matter of pigeon's milk
and strap-oil. I have done so. I may so far
tolerate the last obsolete struggles, the dying
kicks, if I may so speak, of defunct supersti-
tion, as to do it again. But the next occasion
which I am called from my duties to my em-
ployers to be insulted, I can only tell you, Mr.

Bassett, plainly, distinctly, firmly, and irre-
vocably, that I shall be under the painful
necessity of refusing to go, and for the consequences of which refusal, Mr. Bassett, the responsibility will be yours.'

' You've seen no girl ? '

' There's where it is.  I have seen a girl,
and when I asked her if she was looking for
any sort of a baby, she—— But I will
not condescend to inform you of the indig-
nities which, Mr. Bassett, your want of consideration caused me to suffer at her hands—
to say nothing of her tongue.  With your
permission, Mr. President—Mr. Bassett, I
should say—I think that under the circumstances, the most convenient course will be
for me to withdraw.'

' Hold hard, admiral !  I'm sorry if your
ears have had to suffer at the hands of out-
raged propriety, but—alas !—look there—
there, on the sofa—not on the ceiling, man
alive !  Do you call that a joke on the part of
myself and my friends ? '

. ' Why, Lord help us, Mr. Bassett, what
doings are these ? '

' Is it a child ? '

' It's that, sure enough,' sighed the

admiral, who had spent all the indignation he could find, and had to wait for the secretion of a further supply. 'I know—none better. I've seen six to-day, and all my own.'

'Indeed? Then for six reasons, admiral, I appoint you president of this council. Listen, and learn the absolute awfulness of the situation. That child was handed through that window by a young woman of whom we know nothing—neither name, nor address, nor, in one word, anything whatever. And she has, for reasons only known to herself, left it here on our hands. What are we to do? You're youngest present, Urquhart; what do you propose?'

'That is just the vera question,' said Urquhart. 'For, ye see, without experience, 'tis just impossible to know anything at all. We ought to consult with somebody to whom all this has happened before.'

'Thank you very much,' said Charley, 'I'll advertise for such a man. Well, Ronaine?'

'By the powers!' suddenly exclaimed Ronaine, too excitedly to be careful of grammar; 'by the powers! 'tis a She!'

'A girl!' cried Charley, with a start, as if he had never before dreamed that babies

could be otherwise than of the neuter
gender.

'Poor little thing!' said Esdaile, with
scarcely a tinge of coldness, and none of
mockery, in his tone.

Jack Doyle took to chewing the ends of
his big beard. The admiral's weak blue eyes
became weaker and bluer than before.

Why should the doctor's very simple discovery have brought about so sudden a
change in the atmosphere? But so it was,
and they seemed to regard the little sleeping
creature with entirely new eyes. And it may
be safely wagered that nothing of the sort
would have happened had It turned out to be
He instead of She.

'What a blackguard shame!' cried
Ronaine. 'And here are five men—and the
admiral—six men, who don't know what to do
with that mite of a girl! We ought to be
ashamed of ourselves.'

'Yes,' said Bassett. 'We can't let a
woman that is to be grow up in a workhouse
to be Heaven knows what—that's clear, if
nothing else is. We should be less than men.
But the worst of it is—— Of course I've got
sisters, but I should like to see their faces if I

asked their advice about a foundling! Yes,
and when I told them I didn't know the
mother, they'd refer me, most unquestionably,
to the nearest depôt of marines. They're good
women. You know what that means,' said
Charley, with the shrug of those who are still
young enough to fancy they know the world.
'And yet a woman that isn't good won't do
to row in this galley. Oh, if I but knew of
one good woman who would do a good deed!'
he cried, out of the cynicism proper to his
years.

Maybe, if he had occasionally strayed into
the drawing-rooms of Philistia, he might have
known of more than one.

'It is a grand opportunity,' said Urquhart,
eyeing the child like a famished eagle; 'just
grand! Think of the experiment of bringing
up a woman-child without the intervention of
woman-kind! Nothing has been done in that
way since the days of Eve, and that experiment was not wholly complete or satisfactory.
The chance of all chances, for which the
world might have waited for a thousand
years—I wouldn't lose it for a thousand
pounds. We'll be able to observe the limits
of the influence and the determining quality of

sex, and all manner of phenomena that will reveal themselves as time goes on and the lassie gets bigger. To think of the thoughts and the feelings, and the instincts and the passions, all waiting in that wee bit of a sub-ject, like the stops and pipes in an organ, for somebody to play on them and find out all they mean——'

'Ye cold-blooded blackguard!' cried Ronaine. 'Ye'd be cutting the bellows open! Not a bit of it will I stand by an' see that girl vivisected in the name of philosophy, nor any other name. We'll make her just the grandest woman that ever was seen. She's got health—ye can see that, if it's only by the way she's sleepin'—and health means beauty. I'll make a Helen of her, by judicious physical development, to set the world blazin'. Faith, 'tis the devil's own luck she has, to be sure! By the time she's that high, she'll be own daughter to a Lord Chancellor, and the President of the Royal Academy, and the editor of " The Times," and the cousin to a baronet, not to speak of me-self, all rolled out into five—and it's proud of her we'll be that day.'

'But meanwhile,' said Esdaile, ' the Lord Chancellor has never seen a brief, the

P.R.A. is a deputy assistant scene-painter, and the editor of " The Times " is—Jack Doyle. And——'

'And a child,' burst out Jack Doyle, suddenly waking up again, a child's no more fit to be trusted to a set of good-for-nothing, drunken blackguards like us, than I am to be sub-editor of " The St. Giles's Scarecrow." And I say——'

'Holloa, archdeacon,' said Bassett, ' that's a touch too far. But, it is a fact that, whether Urquhart is to turn her into corpus vile, or Ronaine into a phœnix, somebody must meanwhile turn her into a—woman. We can't bring her up by hand. We can pay for her keep—I don't suppose champagne is wanted every day at that age—but whom are we to pay? I'm quite ready to make a compact. We'll put her parentage into commission, and nothing shall be done concerning her, whether by way of experiment or otherwise, save with the unanimous consent and joint action of the whole board. That will give just one chance to Nature. All right, Urquhart, you shall enjoy the experiment of watching the growth of a natural woman to your heart's desire. All right, Ronaine, if we can make her a phœnix—a phœnix she shall be. And all right, Jack, we won't teach her to drink, or to swear, or to be anything misbecoming a modest girl. I like you, Jack Doyle, but I'm not going to be told I'm unfit company for man, woman, or child. But now——'

'I think I heard you say you was inquiring after a good woman, Mr. Bassett,' said the admiral, in a timid and hesitating way. 'They are scarcish articles, to be sure. But I do happen to be acquainted with one——'

'Hear, hear!' cried Charley. 'Go on, admiral. Name!'

'And it occurs to me, Mr. Bassett, that she might not object, if properly asked, to look after the child, and to—and—and—in short, Mr. Bassett, to altogether do for her. She is a good woman, though not without human failings, and lamentably incapable of taking any intelligent interest, or indeed, Mr. Bassett, any interest at all, in public affairs. That is a defect in a woman; but, happily though it may affect her value as a wife to a public man, it leaves her, as a mother, pretty much as she was before. In short, Mr. Bassett, she happens to be my own wife; and I wouldn't take a hundred pounds to go home, and tell her I'd left a fellow-creature, however small, to—to——'

'To the mercies of "a set of good-for-nothing, tipsy blackguards"? Quite right. You're a good fellow, admiral. Take her off to Mrs. Nelson, and here's a five-pound note for cab hire. I suppose that'll be enough to keep a little scrap of a thing like that for a few days. I'll see Mrs. Nelson to-morrow. If matters can be settled to her satisfaction, you must be yourself one of the commission. Gentlemen, we hereby resolve ourselves into a company for executing the office of joint fathers to—to—hang it all! To whom?' .

'And there's not so much as an initial to her back,' said Ronaine, 'unless Mrs. Nelson may find one, and then it wouldn't be her own.'

'She must have a name,' said Esdaile. 'Why not give her one ourselves?'

'Everything's in a name,' said Bassett. 'Marion? Simple, unaffected, poetical, suggestive——'

'Of what?' asked Esdaile. 'It's all you please, except suggestive. Now, you see, she has no name, practically speaking. To us, she is simply a piece of womankind. She

comes to us out of a garden.   In a word, she
is just Eve.   Let her be just—Eve.   That
suggests everything.'

'Ah, but she's more than  just Eve!' said
Urquhart, rather sharply.   'Marion is too
general.   Eve is too universal.   What we
want is the special name to define her precise
relation to the metaphysics of the future.
Psyche—the Archetype of the Human Soul!'

'Call her Physic at once!' said Ronaine.
'Psyche, pooh!   Give her the name of the
biggest woman ye can find.   Zenobia; now
there's a name!   Beat that if ye can!'

'H'm!' grunted Bassett.   'Now, admiral,
what's your notion of a name for a girl?'

'They're all good names, Mr. Bassett, one
and all.   But to my mind, there's no name
you can give a girl comes half-mast high to
Dulcibella.   It's what I'd have called my own
last, if it hadn't been a boy.   Dulcibella's a
beautiful name.'

'Well,' said Bassett, 'let's try for a surname, as there seems some difference of
opinion about the other.   I think Marion
perfect. Eve comes next ; but Zenobia! Well!
But as to the surname.   Let me see.   Smith—
no.   Vavasour—Davenant—no.   Won't do

to give her one of our own. Pitt—Fox
—Buonaparte. Wait a bit; if we've got
vowels enough among our own initials we
might make up an anagram; a joint name.
A good notion, and a new. Let's see. Esdaile
—Urquhart — Nelson — Ronaine — Bassett—
Doyle. Two vowels out of six; that ought
to do. R-U-B-D-E-N : Rubden. Will that do?'

'Hideous!' said Esdaile. 'She'll be
changing it the first chance that comes.'

'Rubned,' Bassett went on, shifting the
letters, 'Burned—by no means. Bruned—
Bruden—Burden——'

'Halte-là!' cried Ronaine. 'Burden—
there ye are; Burden : because she shan't be
one—and good sounding, too.'

'Let me see,' said Bassett again. 'B for
Bassett; U for Urquhart; R for Ronaine; D
for Doyle; E for Esdaile; N for Nelson. Yes,
all there. So be it—Burden. Six names in
one.'

'Zenobia be hanged!' broke in Jack Doyle,
whose mind had been lagging behind, and had
reached no farther than the question of the
christian name. 'Call a spade a spade, and a
blackguard a blackguard, and a girl a girl.
Give her a girl's name. Call her Jane.'

'Well, archdeacon,' said Charley, ' since we can't agree we won't quarrel. If a woman's ever to come between us, she shall be more than a year old. Gentlemen, charge your glasses. Silence for the chair. I call upon you, my most respectable fellow-fathers, to drink all happiness, and so forth, to a young lady of tender years, who is destined, not only to solve all the problems which have puzzled philosophers from Thales to Urquhart, but also, with her beauty and genius, to set the Thames blazing from Brentford to the Nore. We, Patres Conscripti, are chosen as the humble instruments for the bestowal of this paragon upon an undeserving universe, thus returning good for evil, and—and—but my eloquence overwhelms me. In short, gentlemen, I call upon you, as one man, to drink health and happiness to Mistress Marion Eve Psyche Zenobia Dulcibella Jane Burden. May she live as long as her name! From this hour forth, we are Seven against the world. Charles Bassett, Alexander Urquhart, Ulick Ronaine, Richard Esdaile, Horatio Collingwood Nelson, John Doyle, and Marion Eve Psyche Zenobia Dulcibella Jane Burden. Rise. Join hands. Drink. Swear!'

# CHAPTER I

## STANISLAS ADRIANSKI

THADDEUS OF WARSAW, Lara, and all their kith and kin ? Why, they were nothing at all .to Him. He was Romance in person. To begin with, he was a foreigner. He was black-haired and black-browed, and he wore his hair long and his brows in a tragic frown. The drooping moustachios that hid his mouth —possibly to the advantage of the latter— were in themselves a glory. It was hard to decide whether the man owned the moustachios or the moustachios the man. True, cleanliness was neither his forte nor his foible. But interesting and romantic foreigners are privileged from the trouble and expense of soap ; if one washes too much,

one might as well be something in the City—
a bull or a bear.

Not from the City, or from anywhere near
it, came Stanislas Adrianski.  He was a Pole.
What Ireland is to England, such was he to
the world.  His nationality meant a great
deal ; but he was something more even than
a common Pole.  In war he had waved the
sword, in peace he struck the lyre.  He was
a hero, who taught the piano at three shillings
and sixpence an hour ; but he was a hero, an
exiled hero, all the same.  With sallow face,
pathetic black eyes, and long black hair, with
an aroma of lost battles and of the pathos of
patriotic exile about him, no wonder that he
touched a chord in the heart of Phœbe
Burden that had thrilled to no meaner,
shorter, or cleaner fingers since she had
reached the age when such chords are to be
thrilled.  When he spoke English—sur-
prisingly well considering his foreignership—
in his heroically melancholy way, she felt a
tenderness of accent that seemed to say:
' You understand me.  If my country did not
hold my whole heart, a considerable part of it
would be yours.'

She was only a sort of daughter to a

lawyer's copying-clerk, an elderly widower,
always with the wolf at the door ; but she
had a soul above circumstance, and Stanislas
Adrianski had come nearest to its ideal.
Everybody else was so common and so tame.
There were her brothers, as she called them.
She liked them well enough, but they were
rough and common ; even that queer lad
Phil, who liked books a great deal more than
she, so long as they had no poetry in them—
a form of literature at which he turned up
his nose. Stanislas's nose was aquiline, incapable of turning up at anything, serious,
grave, and expressive of power. Phil had
been known to turn up his even at Stanislas,
which made Phœbe feel how easy it is for the
owl to scorn the eagle. The eagle is above
scorn. There were her neighbours, too ; but
they were nobodies, one and all.

Phœbe was not one of those girls, if such
there be, who take no interest in the natural
history of young men. But she was one of
those who rise from the study with an incu-
rious wonder as to what makes it attractive
to other girls. She was 'fond of poetry,' as a
certain immature phase of mind used to be
described by simple people ; she also believed

in it ; and it was a standing marvel to her
how and whence poets obtained their heroes,
until one memorable evening she saw Stanislas
Adrianski walking up and down the next-
door back garden. The snub-nosed, pimply,
pert, vulgar, ignorant and silly race of young
men turned out to have a reason for its existence after all. They were the waste of the
raw material, the unsuccessful experiments
out of which, once in a generation, Nature
turns out a Stanislas Adrianski.

Phœbe had always spent a good deal of
her time in that back garden. It was her
nearest available approach to the picturesque
and the beautiful, for the parks and the
grand shops were not for every day. Not
much fancy is needed to turn a dead bay-tree
into a forest, a fence of broken oyster-shells
into the rocks that line the edge of their
native ocean, and to see distant blue or snowy
hills swelling in the lines on which Mrs.
Goodge, three doors off, used to hang her
linen to dry. As for animal life, there were
more cats behind that row of houses than in
any other quarter of the globe, while, except
on hot Sunday evenings, there were no young
men at all. It was no doubt a kindred,

sympathetic likeness in tastes and fancies that led this exceptional young man to meditate in solitude among the cats, the clothes' lines, and the oyster-shells.

We do not yet know much of Phœbe Burden. For that matter, she did not know much about herself—even a little less, if possible, than we all know about ourselves. But it is clear that a girl who knows how to conjure with oyster-shells is not likely to come across a stranger like this without feeling a touch of natural curiosity. She was not nineteen, so far as anybody could tell; and she found even less trouble in setting up nine romances in nine minutes than in bowling them down afterwards; though she found no particular trouble in that either. It did not strike her that there was any difference between inventing a non-existent hero and giving the hero's rôle to a real young man on the other side of one's own garden-wall, and that wall a low one.

'Suppose,' thought she, after her neighbour, without having seemed to see her, had gone indoors; 'suppose—let me see, what would be the nicest thing to suppose? Suppose I were some day all by myself in the

garden—no ; suppose I were looking out of
the front window, when a party of soldiers,
foreign soldiers they must be, of course,
came marching along the street, led by a spy.
I should know him by his face to be a spy.
They would knock next door, and the officer
and the spy would go in. I should wonder
what was happening, when, all on a sudden,
I should feel my wrist grasped tightly, and,
before I could cry out, I should hear an
agonised whisper of "Save me, my enemies
have discovered me!" What should I do?
He would have seen the soldiers and run up
on to the roof and come down into our house
by the chimney. No ; that would make him
look like a sweep ; he should have, at the risk
of his life, dropped from the edge of the roof
to our top window-sill, and scrambled in that
way. I should look round, thinking what I
should do, when the soldiers would come
thundering at our door. "Search the house,"
I should hear Phil saying. "You'll find
nobody here." "Ah! but we saw him
swing himself in through the top window,"
the spy would answer, and then I should
hear them coming, tramp, tramp, up the
stairs. "There!" I should exclaim, point-

ing to the cupboard under the stairs. In he would go, and I should lean against the door, covering the keyhole and handle, so that the soldiers would never guess there was a door at all. The spy would ask me to stand forward, but I should crush him with a look of scorn. The soldiers would go, and then I should have to keep him in the house without letting anybody know. I should have to pretend to lose the key of the cupboard, and when the man came to fit a new one, I—I—I have it! I shall hamper another lock, and tell him that's the one he was sent for to mend. I shall feed the hunted hero by holding a jug of milk to the keyhole, so that he can suck it through with a straw, and I shall prevent running up the milk bill any higher by going without milk in my tea. Oh! all sorts of things will happen. But one day I shall hear no answer when I speak to him. A horrible thought will come to me that he is dead. I shall break open the door, and find him—gone! How, I shall never know, but some day, twenty years afterwards, or thirty perhaps, when I had forgotten all about the whole thing, a courier would gallop up the street and pull up his horse just in

front of our door. How all the street would
stare! He would ask for Phœbe Burden.
I shall come upstairs, yes, in my very worst
gown. And then he will say, before them
all: " Thanks to you, His Royal Majesty the
King of Spain "—yes, he does look like a
Spaniard—" His Royal Majesty the King of
Spain, while exiled from his throne, escaped
from his enemies and recovered his crown.
I am sent to ask you to be his queen." And
then the courier will turn out to be the king
himself, too impatient to wait for an answer;
and I shall say : " Well, time must show, but
· I should like to be a queen." '

There was not much harm in romances
which might be as reasonably hung upon the
dead bay-tree as upon a stray young foreigner
in a poor suburban lodging. There was no
reason for suspecting him to be so much as a
king's fourth cousin; nor was Phœbe quite
such a goose as to take herself in the least
seriously, except in the matter of wishing to
be a queen. But then it was not upon the
dead bay-tree that this particular romance had
been hung; and it was with a touch of new
self-consciousness that she next went out into
the garden.

Of course we all know that no girl ought ever to feel the slightest interest in any strange young man, to whom she has never spoken and whom she has only once seen. Of course we know that, in good society, such things are never known to happen—that not even schoolgirls throw the most passing thought upon such things. But, alas! Phœbe was not in good society; she was not even a well-brought-up girl, and she had never seen a man quite like Stanislas Adrianski before.

On the other hand, no thought of his speaking to her ever entered her brain, except under purely imaginary and impossible conditions. She wanted a live hero for her own personal poems, and here was one, almost as good as if she had had him made to order.

That was the beginning, and that looked very likely to be the end, and that would have been the end, had not the interesting stranger continued to live next door. She did not make any attempt to find out his name or calling, though that might easily have been done. Perhaps she did not like to face the chances that his name might turn out to be plain John Jones, and that his calling might prove less interesting than that of exiled majesty.

How their first acquaintance came about she hardly knew. May be it is next to impossible for a pretty girl and a fascinating young foreigner to keep a very low garden-wall for ever between them. He never seemed to have anything to do all day but lounge about in company with a cigarette. She was nearly all day at home alone.

A first 'Good morning, miss,' in such a case, is a stone set rolling down a steep hill, gathering force and swiftness out of all proportion to the first impulse that made it go.

Before long she had learned a story that set her whole heart glowing. There was romance in every syllable of such a name as Stanislas Adrianski. He was not a king. But he had a right to call himself count, if he condescended to such vanity, and he was better even than an exiled emperor ; a banished patriot, who had fought and lost for Poland. Of his unhappy country he never spoke but with tears in his eyes : of Russia, never without a heat that woke an answering warmth in Phœbe. It was something to talk with a man who had a Czar for an enemy.

How he lived, considering that his estates were confiscated and that he had no ostensible calling, she did not learn. Perhaps it was by conspiracy. It did not hurt him in her esteem that her rough-tongued and would-be witty brothers, who had seen him about, called him by all sorts of contemptuous nicknames. He was above them ; and it was natural that, as British youths, they should throw stones at whatever they could not understand. Their tone added a dangerous touch of piquancy to a relation that derived half its original zest from being apart from all common things.

There was absolutely nothing to alarm her in the manner of the young man. In point of courtesy, according to her lights, it was everything that could be desired. He was evidently a count, as well as a patriot to the backbone. Sometimes she thought that a touch of sentiment would be a not unwelcome addition to his patriotic tirades. But she never fished for it, and did not think the worse of a patriot for being above such trifles. He flattered her more by talking of himself than either he or she could tell. But the stone had not yet done rolling.

'How it is strange,' said Stanislas, one fine

autumn evening, while she was taking the air on one side of the wall and he on the other; 'How it is strange that I find you here!'

'Why?' asked Phœbe.  'It is much too pleasant out of doors to stay in.'

'That is not who I mean.  I mean, you are as a Princess in a history; you are not of yours, no more as I am of England.  That is strange to me.  I see your father: you are not like him.  I see your brothers: you are not like them.  You are like yourself alone.'

'Yes—I suppose I am like myself, a little.' She coloured slightly at the new excitement of having herself made the subject of talk instead of Poland; and she did not feel inclined to let the topic go.  'But it would be strange if you knew whether I am like my father and my brothers——'

'Am I blind?  No.  I see them, and I see you.  They are of the earth: you are of the sky.'

Phœbe coloured a little more deeply; it was the nearest approach to spoken sentiment that he had ever made, and then the phrase was in itself beautiful poetry: a speech that she was proud to think had never been paid before to any girl.

'I am not of the sky—you may be sure of that,' said she. 'But—if I were like father, or my brothers—that would be strange.'

'Pardon. That is who I do not comprehend.'

'Because—because I have no father, and no mother, and no brothers—because I never had any at all.'

'Ah! You mean you are not one of those?'

'I—I'm afraid—I really don't know who I am; not even my own name. I hope you, as Count, you know, won't think very much the worse of me; but it's true. You won't think it so very dreadful?'

'Dreadful? You mean terrible? No. But you interest me, more as tongue to say. I am glad you are not of those. I am glad I am right. I often say to myself: "She is not of those." So—you know not which you are?'

'No. I belong to a mystery. What it means I do not know.'

'Confide in me. It can be I may tell. Mysteries? They are adorable. I love them; I like them very much indeed. Since Poland is slave, it is the air I breathe. A mystery— and of you!'

'I do not know who I am. . . . . But, when I think of it—if I let myself think of it, and I can't help that, now and then—it makes me fancy thousands of things. . . . . I have lived here all my life ; but I am not **Mr.** Nelson's daughter, and my name is not Phœbe Nelson, but Phœbe Burden ; and that is all I know.'

'But they know ? '

'They ?  Not my—brothers ; and if Mr. Nelson knows, he does not tell.'

'And he brings you up—he keeps you ? He pays ? '

'Ah, that is another mystery !  Four times a year there comes a letter from India with money—for me.'

Stanislas suddenly stopped in his walk, and leaned his arms upon the top of the wall.

'Money—from India—for you?  Is it much, mademoiselle ? '

'A great deal.  It is——'

'Hulloa ! and what the devil,' exclaimed a strong quick voice from behind her shoulder, 'what the devil are Miss Burden's money matters to you?  And what the deuce do you mean, Phœbe, by talking to fellows over the wall at this hour?  Come in.'

This rough interruption, to say the least
of it, came from a big broad young fellow
of not much over one-and-twenty, whose
approach from the back door neither Phœbe
nor Stanislas had perceived. He was not
handsome, though by no means of the contemptible physique which Phœbe Burden
ascribed to young men at large. On the
contrary, had he not been that Phil Nelson
with whom, as with a real brother, she had
grown up from her infancy, she might, perhaps,
have regarded him with favourable distinction.
As things were, she felt herself turn hot and
cold with a sort of shamefaced anger, while
Stanislas, in the coolest manner possible,
lighted another cigarette and resumed his
walk up and down. A hero of romance is
not to be put out by a mere Philip Nelson.

But to be accused of talking to fellows
over a wall, when one is really giving one's
confidences to the sympathetic soul of a
patriot, martyr and hero, is like having one's
higher life suddenly degraded and vulgarised.
Phœbe turned with a temporary submission
to Philip Nelson's rough command; but it
was from a wish to save her hero from rough
insult which might too sorely wound his

sensitive soul—certainly not from any intention of submitting hereafter.

'Phœbe,' said Philip more gently, 'I am
your brother, you know, and it's my duty to
look after you.  What does this mean?'

She looked through the deepening twilight across the wall, and saw the light at the
point of the cigarette vanishing into the house
to which the back garden over the wall
belonged.

'What does what mean?' she asked
quickly.  'What do you mean by insulting a
gentleman before me, and me before him?'

'I didn't mean to listen, Phœbe—I didn't
listen; but I couldn't help hearing.  I'd come
back to tell you of some good news for
myself, thinking you might care—but never
mind that now—and it wasn't good to find
you talking like to an old friend to that
foreign cad next door.  How long have you
known him, Phœbe?  I've a right to know,
and if I hav'n't——'

'You hav'n't,' said she; 'and a count——'

'A count!  Every bagman's a count,
abroad.  And I don't believe that fellow's
even a bagman.'

'I know him.  He is a Polish patriot, if

you know what that means. He is a hero, and I am proud——'

'Hero enough ! He seemed to know, from the way he sneaked off without a word, that my toes felt uncommonly like kicking——A Pole, is he ?—and a patriot ?—and a count ?—and a hero ? Oh, Phœbe, if this happens twice, a Pole, and a patriot, and a count, and a hero, and a cad, and a coward, will have to learn what a common English fist means. There—once for all—come in !'

It may be thought that Philip Nelson spoke with more than a brother's ill-temper, and if he thought this the way to make short work of Stanislas Adrianski, it is certain that he was a fool.

# CHAPTER II

### PHILIP NELSON

A SUDDEN plunge from the warm bed where
we have been dreaming all sorts of vague,
intangible fancies—all the more luxurious
for their being so completely beyond the
reach of sense or reason—into the biting
reality of a half-frozen bath on a winter
morning, is nothing to the sensation of having
the first warmth of one's first romance sub-
jected to such an uncompromising shower-
bath as Philip Nelson's treatment of Phœbe's
back-garden flirtation.   She was not in love
with Stanislas, nor had he, until that evening,
suggested the possibility of his regarding her
as anything more or better than a sympathetic
audience, such as every poet and orator
requires.   But this evening there had been
a tender something in the patriot's manner,
suggestive of the possibilities of her becoming
a living heroine to a living hero.   Nor had

she noticed the sudden access of enthusiasm and the deepening of tenderness which had followed his learning that the money from India, four times a year, was a great deal. For that matter, few women could associate the idea of money with Stanislas Adrianski, or him with it, either as desirer or possessor. If he had put money before Poland, he could have had it ; and that he had it not, everything about him plainly declared.

Philip Nelson's whole conduct, therefore, had been no less unjust than vulgar, and Phœbe could not enough admire the delicacy of the Pole in avoiding a quarrel in the presence of a woman. She was angry with Philip, and all the more for being unable to help being rather afraid of him. He was the only one of her family of whom she was ever afraid ; and she was only too ready, since she had started a romance, to give him the necessary part of villain. And, for that matter, the young man looked fierce and sullen enough to suit the most exigent of heroines, as he marched before her into the house, and bade her follow him.

The interior in which Phœbe had grown up was humble enough, and, being free from every sort of feminine intrusion except her own, was also a rough and ugly one. No wonder she was fond of the back garden, and no wonder she drew an altogether one-sided contrast between out-of-doors and in-doors on this particular evening. Philip Nelson—her brother and yet not her brother —was as unlike Stanislas as one young man can possibly be unlike another. Nobody could dream of making Philip a peg to hang any least rag of romance upon, although, by many eyes, he would be held the better-looking of the two, if only because he was cleaner and more wholesome. That was more than could be said of the Nelsons' parlour, which, though in a girl's charge, did not strike the senses as being either wholesome or clean. But then it had been the common room of a whole herd of rough motherless boys. And what were one girl's hands against so many? For that matter, as her memory only too justly brought up against him, Philip himself, though by far the least riotous of the whole herd, had been one of the most grievous sinners in the matter of litter. He had been that most uncomfortable and most incomprehensible of young men—a serious,

steady, plodding worker in a house where
nobody followed his example any more than
anybody had set it for him. He had one
way, or rather fifty ingenious ways, as Phœbe
knew to her cost, of leaving books, papers,
and mysterious instruments in ʃall sorts of
inconvenient places, and of expecting to find
them, perhaps three weeks afterwards, in the
identical spot where he had left them. He
was given to spend evenings at home, during
which he smoked not over-fragrant pipes
over the production of zig-zags, about which
Phœbe used to feel that she could have de-
signed far more elegant patterns without the
pipe in a hundredth part of the time, and
with no trouble at all.

'Phœbe,' he began again, taking up a
judicial attitude in front of the fireplace—
'Phœbe, I want to know what all this
means.'

'What what means, Phil?' she asked,
more innocently than she felt, as she began
to clear the unsteady round table and to
noisily set out the cups and plates for some
kind of meal.

'Do be plain and outspoken. What do
you mean by letting a stranger—and such

a stranger!—ask you questions about your affairs?'

'I can't help people asking questions,' said she.

'I don't know about that. I suppose a man doesn't ask questions unless he expects an answer. How long have you known this fellow—what's his name?'

'Count Stanislas Adrianski? Oh, I don't know. But why do you talk as if I had been committing some crime? Don't you choose your own friends?'

She was not speaking quite in the manner she would have wished; but it is not easy, without pens, ink, and paper, and an hour or two of preparation, to extemporise the style of a heroine of romance who is being bullied by a high-handed and unsympathetic brother. She felt that she was doing justice neither to herself nor to Stanislas Adrianski. But, always afraid of Phil, she was becoming conscious that she was afraid. In default of the right words and phrases, she was falling back upon the common feminine (and masculine) trick of confusing the issues.

But Phil was much too logical by nature to allow anything of that kind.

'I'm a man and you're a girl,' said he.
'I'm bound to take men as they come ; but I
don't ask them how much money they have
a quarter.  It won't do, Phœbe—it won't do.'

'What won't do ?  And why ?'

'Talking to fiddling foreign counts won't
do.  Picking up chance acquaintances won't
do.  Reading trash won't do.  As for why—
one can't tell a girl everything ; a girl must
trust her elders——'

'By three years ?  Yes, you are that
much older, if I'm really as young as I'm
told.  But you're not old enough to be my
grandfather, Phil, whoever he may have been.
And I should say that Count Stanislas Adrianski is, at any rate, nearer my grandfather's
age than you.'

'Hang the fellow !  As if I couldn't see
through his sort with half an eye !  There's
something contemptible about the very sound
of the fellow's name.  It sounds as if he'd
cribbed it from some East-end play.  And he
suits his name.  If a fellow said to me what
I said to him, I'd have knocked him down.'

'You think you deserve to be knocked
down ?  Perhaps the count didn't think it
worth while.'

Their eyes suddenly met. And, as suddenly, the young man and the young woman who had grown up together from childhood felt that they had been strangers until then. Her fear of him began to change into a curious certainty that this very plain-spoken young man was neither saying what he meant nor speaking as he wished to speak—some hidden imp was telling her that to dwell upon the name of Count Stanislas Adrianski at full length, and with its title, was a sure way of punishing him badly for his interference; and this not because the name or title struck him as really contemptible, but rather the other way. And as for him; what was it that had come to Phœbe that she should show such hitherto unsuspected capacity for being sharp and bitter? He was not thin-skinned; but this was a stab from a needle, which easily pierces what can resist daggers.

But, though triumphing in her last stab, which she felt to be a good one—so good that her pleasure in giving it almost interfered with the careless ease which gives point to scorn—she repented of it almost as soon as it had been made. A flush and frown came over Phil Nelson's face that made her really afraid. It was a look of anger and pain together, of which his face seemed incapable by its very nature.

It was a dangerous moment for her, for it gave her a sense, not only of fear, but of power. She had never seen him thus before, and she was beginning, by some new insight, to guess the cause. Was it possible that she, Phœbe Burden, had in one evening, and without leaving her own door, won the sympathetic interest of an exiled Polish nobleman and made another man downright jealous thereby? Here was the beginning of a real romance, indeed, even if it did no more than end where it began. She could fill up the rest at her leisure, when she found herself alone again. No wonder that Phil Nelson aroused a new interest in her, just as a real stranger would have done. Even the fear was a pleasant thing to feel, as soon as it fairly took its place as a line in the web that her head was weaving. It was Phœbe's first taste of the pleasures of the coquette, and they had a bewildering charm. She took it for romance, just as she had taken Stanislas Adrianski for a hero.

Perhaps she was right. Women consider themselves to be born with—as a gift from Nature to them, and to them alone—an infallible instinct wherewith to understand themselves and men too. And who ought to know better than they? But meanwhile, thanks to Stanislas Adrianski and other back-garden fancies, it was beginning to look as if the brother, who was not a brother, were in a fair way of becoming sport to a girl who was not worth the distraction of his mind from the simplest geometrical problem. He looked likely to find harder problems than there are in geometry before he had done—harder to solve, and less worth solving, or more.

Both flush and frown, however, left his face almost as soon as they had come.

'It is enough to put a fellow into a rage,' he said, almost humbly, as if he were in some sort begging her pardon. 'I'd come home with some good news that I wanted you to know before anybody else; and I will tell it you first, all the same. Only—please tell me, Phœbe, right out, that there's nothing more than common neighbourly acquaintance between you and that fiddling scarecrow. Of course I know there isn't, but——'

'But there is, Phil. There's a great deal
more. I don't object to scarecrows from your
point of view. I very much prefer them to
the crows, who can do nothing but croak and
make a disagreeable noise, and don't mind
their own business, and are generally troublesome. I have the greatest admiration for
Stanislas Adrianski—for Count Stanislas Adrianski, I should say. It is something to have
become a scarecrow, and a fiddler, and—
I forget what else you called him—for the
sake of his country. Would you become a
fiddler and a scarecrow for the sake of
yours?'

'Certainly not!' said Phil. 'Nor would
anybody with a country worth mentioning.
That's all humbug, Phœbe. If a man wants
to serve his country, let him work for her, or
fight for her; you can't do her a pennyworth
of good by loafing about with your hands in
your pockets, and telling women what a fine
fellow you are. They believe you, of course,
and you may end in serving one of your
countrymen by picking up one of them with
a few more pounds than brains. If he was a
barrel-organ man I wouldn't mind; he'd be
in his right place, and ask you for your pence

honestly. But—well, that isn't what I've got
to say. Give me your word, Phœbe, that
you'll have nothing to say to—well, Count—
I won't venture on his name. Give me your
word on that, and you shall never hear of
him again from me.'

This began to sound delightfully like
tyranny. She had been so little ruled that it
would have been almost a pleasure to submit,
if only for the sake of the novelty of the thing ;
and perhaps, if he had known a little better
how such matters are to be managed, he
would have got his own way at one big
stroke, and have kept it for ever after. But
he did not know. And so, for want of just
the right word, or perhaps only the right
look, at the right moment, her mood suddenly
changed, and she broke into a laugh which
took even herself so much by surprise that
she let a teacup fall and break on the
floor.

'Oh, Phil, what nonsense ! Why, father
himself would be the first to laugh at such an
idea. As if I could sit in the house all day
long for fear I should be spoken to over the
wall ! It's like what one reads about nun-
neries and girls in Spain ; and from what I've

read, they're not content to keep on their own
side of the wall.  I am.'

'H'm!  But the count can climb, I suppose, as well as you?  Well, if he does, I
shall know how to tackle him.  But as to you
—you won't give me your word?'

'It would be too silly.  But I'll give you
my word not to ask him to run away with me,
though that wouldn't be bad fun.'

'He might ask you to run away with him.'

'Well, perhaps he will.  Who knows?
But he couldn't do it if I said No.'

'But—you would say No?'

'Phil!  How can I tell?  I should rather
like to be a countess, and——'

'Don't turn a serious thing into a joke,
anyhow.  It is a serious thing.  Here are
you, all alone all day long, with nobody to
look after you, and a strange foreigner, who's
most likely a scamp, with nothing to do but
hang round you.  I wish mother was alive.
I'm not even your brother, Phœbe.  I've no
business to order you.  But it's my business
to tell you what's right and what's wrong, and
to keep scamps out of the road.'

'Why?'

'As if you didn't know that as well as I!'

'But I don't know it, indeed.'

'You don't even want to know,' he said, rather savagely. 'Perhaps if I was a count or a marquis—thank Heaven, I'm only an engineer!—perhaps you would care then.'

'If you were a duke, still more. How do I know that I'm not a duchess myself, Phil? I do begin to think I must be somebody, and Count Stanislas Adrianski says he's sure.'

'How much more stuff has he been saying to you? I—I can only hope you're joking, Phœbe. If you knew how you're hurting me,—when I meant——'

'You don't know who I am. Father doesn't know. I don't know. How do you know that I mayn't be a long-lost queen?'

'I'll put an end to this, anyhow . . . I —I don't suppose for a minute you're anything above us, if one man can be called above another till he makes himself so. Fine ladies don't get lost in Gray's Inn Garden. Poor people's babies get lost anyhow and anywhere; and as for me—I don't care. If you turned out a duchess, you'd be plain Phœbe Burden to me all my days. I want to keep you good and safe—that's all; and I believe I can do that as well as a duke, and better . . . I've just got the chance I've been working and waiting for. The firm have asked me to go out and take charge of part of a line we're going to construct in Russia. It's a big thing for me—a thing that older and better men would give one of their ears for. So it's an honour, too ; but it makes me able to ask you something that I've been wanting ever since I was eighteen. I shall come back with money, and, if I do my work well, I shall have my foot well on the ladder. It oughtn't to be long before I'm able to relieve father from— well, from work, and to help all the boys, and to live my own life too ; but I shall be away, you see, all the time, and—— Of course, I can't go on, all that way off, without being certain about things. Just say one plain word, out of your heart, Phœbe. I want to work and live for you. Am I to, or——'

Phœbe could only open her eyes at him— they were large by nature—in sheer, down-right, honest amaze. She knew he was angry and jealous, and that she was the cause ; but this was a very different kind of thing. She very nearly let another teacup fall.

Here she had been, growing up into young womanhood and young manhood with Phil,

the heaviest and gravest of the whole household, and had fancied him married to zig-zags,
whereas, as he now declared, he had been
seeing her face in their contortions and
dislocations for years !

Well, perhaps it is as easy to see a real
girl's face in Asymptotes and Parabolas as to
find a romance hanging on a clothes'-line.
She was only too quick at fancies when they
did not touch her heart, and something of the
sort came into her mind in a vague way that
half touched her and half made her smile.
But to marry Phil ! Only the strangeness of
the notion saved it from being downright
absurd. How could she dream of herself as
the wife of a man whom she had always, even
while half fearing him, looked down upon as
a brother, and who spoke insultingly of heroic
causes and of the heroes who gave up all
things for them, and made the question of
marriage itself turn upon ways and means?

He had not even said one tender word to
her ; had not even told her that he loved her.
Tenderness had come into his voice, and love
into his eyes ; but that was not the way.

He saw her surprise, and was surprised.
It did not occur to him that his one thought

for years might possibly seem new to anybody else in the world. He knew he had been speaking awkwardly and terribly out of season.

As he came home from the office, full of hope and of his new good fortune, he had been painting, in his lover's fancy, a very different scene. He would find her alone, and would share with her his feast of honour and success till the feast should not fail to have a yet sweeter end.

Nobody will be much amazed to find a plodding, practical, prosaic, slow-minded man in love with a girl like Phœbe, rather than with one of his own kind. It was likely enough that he had learned to care for her because of her faults and follies, and by dint of for ever finding fault with them. But his surprise at her surprise was certainly a little surprising.

'Do you want to think of it?' he asked, slowly but anxiously. 'You know I never can say half what I want to—but—will you be my wife when I come home? And—and—now, Phœbe, do you know why I want to keep you out of harm's way?'

'I—oh, Phil, indeed I hardly know what

you mean! No—indeed it can't be. I should never make a wife—for you. Please, Phil— pray don't think of such a thing any more. I'm so glad you've got what you want. I'm so sorry you're going away. But——'

' " No ? " For Heaven's sake, Phœbe——'

' No, Phil. I suppose the shortest word's best—with you.'

' Phœbe—for Heaven's sake,' he said sud- denly, ' tell me it's not that confounded Pole that's in the way ! '

It was the most idiotic speech he could have made—it made her feel the infinite dis- tance that lay between her and Phil. And it sounded to her ears even a little insulting. It was again dragging her secret, unspoken, undefined romance into coarse light and vulgar air.

' Nothing's in the way but myself,' said she, also with rather too much heat to be reassuring. But ' No, Phil,' she said again more gently. ' That's all. That's my last word. There, don't look so angry !—here's father or some of the boys,' she said as a knock sounded at the street-door. ' Father— he'll be so glad to hear of your good news ! '

' It's not good news at all,' said Phil. ' It's

bad news. I shall take it, of course—for the sake of the others—but—I won't tell him now. . . And,' he said to himself, as he left the room so as to escape before the door opened, ' it is that Pole. And to leave Phœbe to a cur like that, who won't even let out when a man insults him to his face before a woman—that shan't be.'

Love, in Phil Nelson's case, was obviously quite consistent with a decidedly low opinion of the good sense and steadiness of the girl whom he wanted to marry. He had told himself that he would set himself to cure her faults, and he had tried: and he would not have loved her half so jealously, or so patiently, or so angrily, or so deeply, if she had lost the least of them.

# CHAPTER III

### WINE, WOMAN, WAR

PHŒBE did not look in the least like a girl who was fresh from her first flirtation with one young man and from her first offer from another, as she gave her last touches to the tea-table and then went to open the street-door.

Phil's lovemaking had been much too awkward to satisfy the romance which her Polish hero had for the first time set vibrating at the touch of real living fingers, while her back-garden experiences had not as yet become part and parcel of her common life indoors. It was still one Phœbe who dreamed dreams, and another Phœbe who made tea. So she was just as cool as if nothing had happened at all as she opened to one who looked as little like Phil's father as he looked like hers, even though he was really the one, and not the other.

The eighteen years or so which had changed Phœbe from a baby into a girl old enough for flirtations and offers had dealt kindly with Horatio Collingwood Nelson.

He was evidently one of those men with an abnormal faculty for standing still. He still looked less like an elderly man than like a sort of fossilised boy.

His hair was lank, thin, and grizzled, but his mild blue eyes beamed from a face without the sign of a wrinkle; his smile retained its infantine weakness, and his wrists their old-fashioned schoolboy trick of projecting limply far beyond the frayed edges of his sleeves.

Life had not gone well with him on the whole, for he made a bad widower, and all his boys had been troublesome from their cradles, except Phil. But they had tumbled up somehow; and their father, so far from seeming crushed by care, had kept up a jauntiness of bearing strikingly out of keeping with the cheap and threadbare shabbiness of his clothes. His very hat had an air of saying :

' I am second hand, and was a bad one from the beginning; but whenever I'm put on, I cover brains.'

' All the boys still out ? ' he asked, in a voice that he had evidently tried to make strong and manly by pitching it as high as it would go,

and rather puffingly, as if time had found out
one weak point about him after all. ' Ah,
boys will be boys !  I was ; and the old block
mustn't complain of the chips—eh ?  Well,
Phœbe, we'll have a carouse together, you and
me.  You shall put in an extra spoon for the
pot, and we'll make it a regular port-wine
night—the boys shan't have all the fun.'

He hung up his hat on a peg behind the
door, rubbing his face all over with his coat-
sleeve, and sat down at the tea-table.

It was not often that he had the pleasure
of getting away early from his office and finding nobody at home but Phœbe ; for Phil,
particularly, was the sort of son of whom a
father, with the least touch of the prodigal
about him, stands in awe.

With Phœbe, on the contrary, he had a
certain sympathy of character ; for though
incapable of seeing mountainous landscapes
in his neighbours' wash, he had his own ways
of looking at things, and they were not much
more real than hers.

' I wish I'd thought of bringing home a
pint of shrimps,' said he.  ' But then I never
thought of not finding any of the boys, and a
pint wouldn't go far among them.  There's

one good thing, though, about not having things—one can make it what one likes. As we haven't got shrimps, we'll make it lobsters. You like lobsters, Phœbe ? '

' Very much indeed,' said she.

' Then, as we haven't got shrimps, we'll think of lobsters. I've got one particular lobster in my mind that I saw coming along. I wish you'd seen it too, Phœbe ; you'd have enjoyed your tea ever so much more. I'd have bought it, in spite of the boys, if it had been just after quarter-day instead of just before. Another cup of tea, if you please. We'll make it champagne this time. I'm in good spirits to-night, as you may perceive. I wonder —I wonder if you know how to keep a secret, Phœbe ? I wonder, now, if you can ? '

' A secret, father ? I should like to know a secret. Is it—is it about me ? '

' You ? Bless my soul, no ! Why should there be secrets about you ? No ; it's about me.'

For a moment the wild thought crossed her mind that her so-called father might be going to give his boys a stepmother.

There was something so especially genial about him this evening, combined with such an obvious pleasure at the absence of the terrible Phil, that, being a girl, she could not help the fancy that he might have been doing by somebody as Phil had been doing by her, and with better success than Phil had obtained.

But then, who could it be that would be willing to unite herself with Horatio Collingwood Nelson, at his time of life, and become stepmother to a batch of rough lads without enough money for house-keeping?

'What is the secret, father?' she asked with exactly the quantity of curiosity he had intended to enjoy.

'Ah, woman—woman—woman! Another cup of tea before it's got to be watered, and then you shall guess twenty times, What I am!'

Many different people would have given different, if not absolutely inconsistent, answers to that question, when asked of Horatio Collingwood Nelson.

Some would have said, 'A fool.' Others, while not altogether denying the fool, would have qualified it by 'knave.' Some would have said, 'A man with a genius for deceiving himself.' Others, 'One with a not inconsiderable talent for deceiving other people.'

I fear that, if the question had been put to Phil, duty would have forbidden him to speak, while truth compelled him to hold his tongue.

And yet a real fool would have been more careworn, and a knave should not have been driven to go without shrimps when he wanted them. He had, at any rate, the wisdom that bears daily troubles with a light heart and a straight back, and the honesty that, when it cannot get shrimps, is content to sup on imaginary lobster.

As for Phœbe, she took him as she found him, and even had a sort of faith in him. Nobody else ever played with her at making believe. And, lover or lobster, the game was very much the same.

'I'll guess forty times, if you like,' said she, for she really liked guessing, and never looked at the end of a novel before she had reached the end of the first volume. 'They have made you a prince in disguise!'

'A prince! Bigger than that, a long way!'

'Bigger than a prince?' she asked, rather surprised that her intended stretch of humour had fallen short of reality. 'You can't mean

that Mark and Simple have made you one of
the firm?'

'Catch them at it! And catch me selling my independence—British independence,
mind you!—for the privilege of having my
name painted black on a white ground!
Besides, I've never been articled; so I
couldn't, however willing. No. Something
that Mark and Simple couldn't be if they
tried.'

'It really is something big, then; very big
indeed!'

'Very, very, very big indeed!'

'It's true, then. You are going to be
married? Oh father! to who?'

'Married! Bless my soul! As if being
married was a particularly big thing! Why,
anybody can get married, Phœbe. It's done
every day. I did think it a big thing when I
married your—I mean the boys' mother; and
it did turn out a big family. But no, Phœbe,
there are certain positions in which a man has
to give up that sort of thing, and to make
sacrifices for—if you were a man you'd understand what he'd have to make sacrifices for.
I—I have been unanimously elected Grand
President of the Associated Robespierres.

There ! That's what I am. And I'll take one
more cup of tea—

> ' Aye, fill.(though envious stars may frown)
>   With blood-red wine the cup—
> We mean to shake the tyrant down
> And knock the freeman up ! '

Phœbe had heard all her life of a series
of associations with various names at which
her father had been in the habit of spending occasional evenings, especially when, as
happened just four times a year, he had more
money in his pocket than at ordinary seasons.
She had a general idea that he was considered
a great orator—not that she had ever heard
him address a much larger audience than
herself (for his sons silenced him), but that
he had given her to understand as much
whenever they were alone together and he
was in a confidential mood. She had supposed, in her innocence, that these for the
most part fiercely-named societies were but
forms of the excuse which men past their
boyhood seem to require for making themselves a little more comfortable than they
find possible at home. But this appeared to
be something very special indeed, and his
emphasis gave his burst into verse a flavour

of reckless grandeur. Her father was, of course, no Stanislas Adrianski. Stanislas, she was sure, would never have stooped from his pedestal to a lobster, or have distinguished himself by tossing off five cups of tea at a sitting. But one does not require one's father to have the fascination of an actual hero and possible lover; enough if a common detestation of something or somebody—tyrants, the income-tax, blackbeetles, it matters not what—forms a link of fellowship between them. She had built up her romance upon the basis of a cruel father. But a sympathetic father, and a gloomy, stern, and jealous rival in the person of Phil, would be still better.

'I am so glad!' said she. 'Tyrants are horrid people! When one thinks of Poland, it is enough to make one want to have them killed. Is it anything to do with Poland— these Associated——'

'Bless my soul! Why, if you're not a chip of the old block! Wonderful — the influence one gets over minds before one knows where they are! Just think—here have I been doing my best to bring up my own boys, and there isn't one that knows the difference between a fool's-cap and a cap of liberty. And Phil's the worst and stupidest of them all. And here's a girl that can't hear of me being grand president without feeling her blood boil! Poland? Rather! I don't know what we should do sometimes for the tail of a speech without the knout, you know, and the Czar, and the exiles of Siberia—Elizabeth, you know. We're going to begin with ourselves—first come, first served—but the freedom of England means the freedom of the world. If Robespierre had begun with England instead of abroad, poor fellow, he might have been among us now. I mean to begin with England. But I sha'n't stop there, not at all. I shall go to Russia too, and give them a bit of my mind. Haven't you got just one more squeeze of tea ? '

' Phil's going to Russia,' said Phœbe.

' Eh ? '

' Yes ; his firm is sending him out to some railway——'

' Just what he's fit for. I hope he won't make a muddle with the tickets, or call out the wrong stations, that's all! No, I suppose they've found out he'd never have done any good at home. Well, families have to grow up and break up, and go all over the world ;

we mustn't complain. And between you
and me, Phœbe, Phil isn't the sort to make a
happy home. A sort of calculating boy—no
interest in politics, and no genius for anything. I don't like those calculating natures
—always wanting to know if a herring and a
half costs three halfpence, how much you'd
have to pay for a penny bun. I like blood
and fire, like me and you. I like wine, and
woman, and war. Ah, that'll be a first-class
toast and sentiment for the A.R.—the Associated Robespierres! Wine, woman, war! War,
wine, woman! How'll it best go? Let me
see. First, wine; second, woman; third,
war. That's the general run of things.'

Whence it may be taken that he was not
quite so great a fool as some thoughtless
people considered him.

'I wish, Phœbe,' said he, after a pause,
while he drained the milk-jug; 'I wish you
were a man.'

'Why?' asked Phœbe. 'I think—I think
I'm just as well as I am. Men don't seem
worth much—except one or two.'

'That's true. But if you were a man,
you could be an A.R.—an Associated Robespierre.'

'What should I have to do?'

'Oh, make speeches, and sing songs, and make tyrants tremble. You'd like it, Phœbe; and so should I. You're worth all the boys put together, though you're not my child and they are. All the same, you're most like me. Phil's his mother all over. She never could bear politics. She used to say it meant the public-house; and she was always thinking of the price of chops, and had no more poetry in her than—than Phil. She was a good woman, though, and did her duty, as my great namesake used to say. But I'm the Father of your Mind.'

'I wonder,' she said with a sigh—'I wonder if I shall ever know who I really am?'

'I hope so, my dear. Anyhow, it's clear you're no common sort of a girl.'

'And you don't even know who sends that money four times a year?'

'It comes, don't you see; it comes, and it would be very bad manners to enquire. Never look a gift-horse in the mouth, Phœbe. The horse might take to kicking, you see. No, no. You leave that to me. What makes you ask me about that now, eh? You never did before.'

'Oh, but I have—many a time. I've often wondered, and wondering has made me think hundreds of things.'

'That's curious—so it has me! Sometimes I've thought you might be a young duchess; but then, I've thought to myself, the aristocracy don't, as a general rule, send out their babies for a walk in Gray's Inn Gardens. But then, your poor mother—I mean my poor wife—used to say your clothes and things were as nice as if you'd been the Princess Royal—only you couldn't have been that, you see. There's no knowing. An uncommonly lucky girl you've been, and to-night you've made me proud of you.'

Meanwhile thought Phœbe: 'A girl with a strange mystery about her disguises herself and becomes an Associated Robespierre. She becomes their chief, and leads them to battle, and makes Poland free. Then she turns out to be a Polish duchess, and so they make her their queen. And Count Stanislas Adrianski—— '

She left her thought unfinished, although it was a real waking thought, and not a dream. It is true that she was not acquainted with the military capacities or proclivities of

the Associated Robespierres, and she forgot
to notice the incongruity of leading their new
grand president to battle. The thought,
therefore, was hardly wise. And yet, what
wise man who knows the world does not
every day coin fancies that are scarcely so
sane, whenever he has a minute or two to
spare?

Alas! if the whole truth must be told,
the real fool of an evening whose events, as
seen with Phœbe's eyes, ranged through the
whole sphere of fancy and feeling, was not the
clerk, who could feel greater than emperors
upon a pot-house throne, nor Phœbe herself,
nor the Polish exile, who may be taken to
know pretty well what he wanted in the
matter of a pretty young woman with a
quarterly income; it was Phil Nelson, who,
with the world before him, had committed
himself to the one idea that he could never
be happy unless he married a girl who seemed
to have a bundle of weeds for a heart and
feathers for brains. He did not even attempt
to invent an excuse for his folly. He knew
her faults by heart; and yet he did not say,
' I won't even think of her faults,' as so
sensible a young fellow ought to have done.

His great piece of news had become bitter, and instead of looking forward to Russia as a land of healthy change and forgetfulness, he —though unable to draw back from employment that meant independence and might mean fortune—felt a dread of it as a place where he would spend half his working hours and all his leisure in jealous thoughts of Phœbe. 'Even if she wrote to me,' thought he, when, having heard his father safely settled at tea, he went quietly out of the house and strode along the neighbouring streets—'even if she writes to me, I shan't trust her letters. She'll be safe to tell me everything except just what I want to know. If there isn't Stanislas Adrianski in every line, I shall be sure she's hiding his name. If she mentions him, I shall be safe to think it's because he's uppermost in her mind ; unless, indeed, it's to tell me that he's got hard labour for swindling. No, she can't be so bad as to take up with the first dirty foreigner that talks to her over a wall. But then she is such a child! She's enough to make one think sometimes that she hasn't got her fair share of brains, with the nonsense she thinks and the trash she reads. If ever I have a daughter, I hope to goodness she won't be like Phœbe. But—but—but——'

Thought lost itself in the consciousness that he loved her, faults and all, with all his heart and soul; and that he would cease to be himself if he ever ceased to love her, faults and all. He did not even wish that he could cease to love her. But it thus felt unbearable to leave her to the fascinations of a man who, he felt by instinct, was not the less dangerous to a woman for being despicable in the eyes of a man. What was he to do? He felt as if he were two selves—one urging him to throw Russian railways to the winds rather than leave the field open and unwatched to his rival; the other and more manly self telling him that he must not allow the trust of life and work and duty to himself and his house to be tossed about by the idle breath of a girl.

'What am I losing by going away?' he asked. 'Only the miserable pleasure of a spy; I can't even guard her unless I sit upon that wall all day long. And then girls like Phœbe, and fellows like that, would cheat me; and she'd end by hating me. But—a year of eternally seeing a picture of those two and that wall! I shouldn't always see it if I stayed at home.'

It was the practice for the Nelson boys, when not out in a body, to stay up for one another, so that the latest might have a certainty of being let in by the latest but one. As a rule, though Phil kept the latest hours of all, he spent them at home, but to-night he was the very last to come home, so tired out by hard walking that he had given up thinking, and that even his jealousy had grown dull.

'Hulloa!' exclaimed the youngest brother, Dick, as, after a good deal of fumbling with the chain, he opened the door, ' here's old Sobersides been out on the spree! Now you've found out what it's like, p'r'aps you'll do it again! Blessed if you aren't as drunk as a lord! Hold up, old fellow; I'll hold you up; I know that sort of thing.' And so, apparently, he did; for, though he spoke plainly enough, he lurched against Phil so heavily as nearly to throw him over.

'And this is the house where she's been brought up, poor child!' thought Phil, more tenderly and more wisely, as he by no means tenderly pulled Dick together. 'No woman to see to her—father what he is—and we what we are. I suppose she's drawn to anybody that's different from us. Foreigners don't get drunk, I believe. But—Hulloa! what's that?'

'Cats, I s'pose,' said Dick, recovering himself from a lurch that sent the banisters creaking up to the highest floor.

But cats are soprani; they do not sing light Italian music with tenor voices in finished style. Cats, it is true, perform their music mostly in back gardens, and it was from a back garden that this unfamiliar music came. It was a fine serenade, finely sung to the thrum of a guitar.

Phil had no more ear for music than Dick, but he could put two and two together better than most men.

'No, foreigners don't get drunk; but foreigners waul, and foreigners strum!' he exclaimed deeply though not loudly. 'That's their notion of love-making'; and in a moment he had unbolted the back door, was out into the back garden, and before the eyes of Dick, who had staggered after him, was seen, in the full light of the moon, breaking a guitar upon the head of its owner. 'Take that, and that, and that!' said Phil, loudly this time, as well as deeply. It was an unspeakably delightful moment. He had been unconsciously longing for a chance of breaking something upon Stanislas Adrianski's head, and now it had come. 'Take that, for waking people up with your caterwauling. If you want my name, I'm Philip Nelson. I'll teach you to sing'; and down came the guitar again.

'Give it him, Phil!' cried Dick from the doorstep. 'That's always the way,' he speculated, being far gone in the philosophical stage of liquor. 'When a Sobersides like Phil does go on the spree—well, he goes.'

# CHAPTER IV

## CHANGE FOR AN ARCHDEACON

' BASSETT ! '

' Lawrence ! '

' By Jove, old fellow, who'd have thought of seeing you ? '

' The same to you, old fellow. But we must look sharp if we don't mean to be left behind. Here's an empty first-class—in with you ! '

They were two young men who had just crossed from Boulogne to Folkestone, and had just managed not to be too late for the same train to town. Lawrence was plain-featured, lean, and bronzed ; Bassett was not unlike that namesake of his who had, a generation ago, lived in Gray's Inn Square, only his style was less languid and more manly. They had settled themselves comfortably, and had taken out their cigar-cases, when, just as the train was under way, another late passenger found just time to throw himself into an opposite corner.

'Do you mind our smoking, sir, as this is not a smoking compartment?' asked Bassett politely, and pausing while in the act of lighting. 'I'm rather particular, you see, about my fellow-travellers' tobacco, and always smoke where other people mustn't, whenever I can.'

His easiness and readiness of address were also characteristic of that Charley Bassett who he could not possibly be, unless, indeed, time had stood even more still with the amateur Bohemian than it had done with the admiral. The stranger's eyes rested upon him rather curiously for a moment before he answered indifferently—'It won't make any difference to me,' and then betook himself to the pastime of looking out of the window. The two young men noticed that he was an uncommonly tall and powerfully-built man, well on into middle age, with a large beard of mingled brown, red, and grey, and a complexion more deeply bronzed than that of Lawrence, but as he looked grave, heavy, and ungenial, and was evidently in no humour for talk, they soon ceased to notice a presence which would not, in any case, have been a restraint upon theirs.

'If I'd been asked where you were, Lawrence,' said Bassett, 'I should have said India, and if I'd been asked what part of India, I should have pleaded Not Guilty of geography. You've not been out there very long? I'm glad to see you, anyhow. All right, I hope? By Jove, barring the brown, I should know you anywhere!'

'It's as odd as it's lucky, old fellow, my tumbling over you the first hour of my coming home. But how was it we didn't meet on board the boat?'

'Why, for the best of all reasons. I was —but don't ask me to speak of it. I always am. My notion of absolute misery is being on board a small steamboat in a rolling sea for two deadly hours. It's an ignominious confession to make to a fellow like you, but I really am a splendid sailor—on shore. Why don't you engineering fellows get that tunnel done?'

'And what are you doing with yourself? No—I don't mean smoking. I see that, but——'

'Oh, nothing very particular. I've just

been walking up a Swiss hill or two with
Aubrey. I walked him off his legs, and he
walked me off mine. Aubrey of Merton, you
know. I left him in Paris, risking his chance
of a fellowship by mooning about with his
prettiest cousin. He's a good fellow, though,
all the same.'

'You missed your chance, of course, in
the regular way?'

'Quite in the regular way. The governor
made a fuss about loss of time and money,
but he never means much when he talks like
that, and as soon as he'd paid the bills he was
just the same as ever. I'm hanging out in
town just now. I'm supposed to be reading
for the woolsack.'

'Going to the bar? You?'

'That's the governor's idea. Of course, I
sha'n't practice, but the governor has his
notions, and—between you and me, Lawrence
—I think he wants to be able to keep an eye
on my goings on. I proposed I should go
into Capel's chambers—Capel of Trinity, you
know; he's got no briefs, but I'd sooner idle
about with him than any man I know, barring
you. However, the governor asked about
Capel, and as he couldn't hear anything about

him from anybody except me, he sent me to
an old friend of his own, a priggish sort of a
Scotchman, named Urquhart, who's said to
be going to be a judge some day. He is a
judge already—of old port; but that's the
only thing I like in him. So I turn up at his
chambers once a week if I've got nothing
better to do, and I don't think the governor
knows anything more about me than if he'd
given the hundred guineas to Capel. Queer
fellows the friends of the governor's youth
must have been, if Urquhart's a specimen!
I'm going to town now for the beginning of
term. Where are you going to put up?
Will you take a shakedown with me? I'll
try and show you a thing or two—if everything isn't tame to a fellow that's been stick-
ing pigs and shooting tigers, or punkahs, or
whatever you call them out there.'

'I've never shot a punkah! By Jove,
you're a lucky dog—only an hour or two of
work a week, if you feel inclined for it, and a
governor who'll pay all your back debts
without so much as winking! Mine didn't.
He told me to go and wipe off the score off
my own bat.'

'Why, he must have been another of the

governor's youthful friends. That was a
d—— well, it wasn't nice of him, anyway.
Well, we'll talk about that another time. I
am born with a silver spoon, and what's the
good of a spoon but to help one's friends?
I was telling you about Urquhart. He makes,
I should say, four or five thousand a year at
least, and I don't believe his tailor gets a ten-
pound note out of the scramble. And he
travels on penny boats and knife-boards. You
don't have fellows like that out in India, I
know.'

'Well,' said Lawrence, 'barring the archdeacon—no.'

'The archdeacon? Oh, a parson—parsons
are different, you know.'

'But the archdeacon isn't a parson. Why
he's called the " archdeacon " nobody knows,
unless it's because he isn't like one. But then
they might just as well have called him a
bishop at once. Archdeacon isn't a common
nickname for a man. You've never heard of
the archdeacon? Why, he's one of the
characters of Bengal.'

'What does he do? You see we are not
in the way of hearing much about Bengal—
except that it's hot, and grows curry-powder.

In what way is this famous archdeacon
queer?'

'In every way,' said Lawrence. 'He's
been out some twenty years, and has never
been home. He's never even taken a holiday,
or been to the hills. He was never seen
speaking to a woman under fifty years old;
and we haven't many old women to speak to.
He didn't come out in the service, but in the
newspaper line; and, somehow, he's managed
to get rich, while other fellows find it a stiff
thing to save a rupee for themselves, let alone
their duns,' he added with a sigh. 'I don't
know what he makes, but it's a big thing;
nor quite how he makes it; but he's so well
known that I shrewdly suspect him of pluck-
ing game better worth it than I am. Maybe
I'll try the experiment some day, when sixty
per cent. mayn't hurt me so much as it would
now, or when things get too tight to manage
any other way. And all the time they say he
doesn't spend three thousand a year—rupees,
I mean; three hundred pounds. And think
of that in India! He must be a regular Jew
—perhaps he is one; and for all his money-
making he's never been known to give away
a brass sou, or to subscribe to anything. In

fact, though men don't know him personally, or don't want to seem to, he's famous for being the meanest beast in all Bengal.'

' And may I ask,' said a deep, slow voice from the corner by the opposite window, ' if you are personally acquainted with the archdeacon ? '

' I ? No,' said Lawrence a little stiffly, and rather put out by this interruption on the part of a stranger whose presence had been clean forgotten. ' I've never even seen him.'

' Then let me advise you,' said the stranger quietly, ' not to judge by hearsay of men whom you do not know. I do know the archdeacon, as you call him. And—though he is no favourite of my own—I know enough to know that you are blaming him for what are not his faults, and leaving his real faults unblamed. He's got real ones enough ; nobody knows that better than I. But——'

' I'm sure I beg your pardon, sir,' said Lawrence, frankly enough. ' I like to hear a man stand up for his friends behind their backs ; it isn't too common. And I'm glad to hear the archdeacon has got a friend to stand up for him. I certainly don't know him, so I daresay you're right and I'm wrong. I was only talking common gossip. Is it long, may I ask, since you were in Bengal? Try one of my cheroots, Bassett.'

'I was in India a month ago,' said the stranger. 'And, if I may ask a question,' he asked abruptly, 'I have just heard you call your friend by a name that once meant a great deal to me. And your face too,' he went on, turning to the other, 'reminded me of your name as soon as I saw you. Can you be any relation to Bassett—Charley Bassett, we used to call him—who once lived in Gray's Inn? But you wouldn't know anything about that; it must have been before you were born.'  •

The young man was not yet old enough to mistrust, on principle, a casual stranger in a railway-carriage who claims old acquaintance with one's family; nor, for that matter, was this stranger's manner of a nature to inspire distrust in any ordinary mind. He spoke with real interest, and without any touch of the geniality which puts the prudent on their guard.

'My name is Bassett; and my father's name is Charles—Sir Charles Bassett, of Cautleigh Hall. Did you ever know him? Perhaps I may have heard him mention you?'

'You are strangely like my old friend; but he was not the baronet, nor likely to be. There was a Sir Mordaunt Bassett, and my friend was some sort of a cousin——'

'My father succeeded Sir Mordaunt; though only a cousin, as you say, there were some unexpected deaths which made him the next heir.'

'I see. . . . And Urquhart; that was another name that we both used to know. So Charley Bassett has become a baronet and Urquhart a great lawyer? Things seem a trifle changed all round. . . . Yes, Mr. Bassett; I did know your father, better than I knew most men, before you were born, and when he no more thought of being Sir Charles Bassett than I do of being—Sir John. It's odd I never knew it; but I don't know—it isn't odd, when I come to think of it, at all. The odd thing is, that the first face I have seen in England should be Charley Bassett's son. Did you ever hear your father speak of Jack Doyle?'

'Well, no; I can't say I ever did,' said young Bassett, after a slight attempt to re-member the name. 'But my father must have had lots of friends of whom I never heard.

And I have no memory for names. I shall never make a case lawyer.'

'Nor of Dick Esdaile? Nor of Ronaine?'

'Never.'

'Well, things do seem a trifle changed. You mean to say you never heard the story of the child with six fathers?'

Young Bassett stared, as well he might; and his friend Lawrence followed his example, though less openly.

'I never heard the story of the child with six fathers,' said he. 'I say, Lawrence, that must be an uncommonly wise child, if the saying's true.' It seemed to him unlikely that a story of unknown date, connecting his father with an uncertain number of old friends and so remarkable a child, should turn out either pleasant or amusing, and his original respect for the size, strength, and quiet bearing of his fellow-traveller was beginning to be touched with very natural suspicion. 'I suppose,' he said, without any of the cordiality due to one's father's old friends, 'I suppose that you are one of those names—Ronaine, Esdaile, or Jack Doyle?'

'I am Jack Doyle. I should think Sir Charles Bassett will remember my—name.

But as he has never mentioned it, never mind.'

And then he fell back into silence, which continued till the train reached London, and a formal 'Good-evening' parted him from the two young men.

'That seemed a queer customer, Lawrence,' said Ralph Bassett. 'The governor does seem to have known a few queer fish when he was young. But I suppose we all do before we settle down.'

'Queer? Queerer than you think, old fellow, by a long way.'

'Why—what do you mean?'

'You noticed how he stuck up for the archdeacon? That was queer to begin with. And then how he got so interested in your father that he fell off his guard; for he was on his guard. As he told you his name, why didn't he say at once, "I'm the archdeacon," like a man? Didn't I happen to tell you that that infernal money-lending vermin's name is Doyle—John Doyle, alias the archdeacon, alias the deuce knows what besides? Yes, he's all that, and I didn't put things half strong enough in the train; but I do now. And what's he doing in England at

last, and asking after Charles Bassett, and half
losing his head when he hears your father has
become a baronet and the richest commoner
in Lincolnshire? And those other men he
named—other poor devils, no doubt, whom
he once had under his thumb, and may also
have got to be worth hunting up again after
all these years? And asking you about a
child with six fathers—it doesn't mean nothing,
you may be sure. Of course it'll be all right,
but, all the same, old fellow, drop a line to
Lincolnshire, and let it be: " 'Ware arch-
deacons—look out for squalls." '

' Are you in earnest, Lawrence? Nonsense. What should my father know of a
usurer from Bengal? '

' Nonsense, a hundred to one; but there's
the one chance it mayn't be. Of course it
will be all right. Your father, I suppose, is
rich enough to snap his fingers; but then that
sort of snapping attracts flies and sharks too.
Perhaps your father may have borrowed a
hundred or two in old times—who knows? '

' I wish I'd asked him,' said Ralph, ' to tell
me the story of the child. No, I don't, though
—it would have been like pumping and spy-
ing. I'll ask the governor if he knows what it

means.    You are a bit of an old woman,
Lawrence, now and then.   There isn't one of
my name who has a ghost of a cause to be
afraid of a living man, except of an examiner
in the schools.'

'But there's no man of any name,' said
Lawrence, 'who hasn't had cause to be afraid
of a woman, and you can't have a story of a
child without having a story of a woman——'

'Of an old woman, and that's yourself,'
said Ralph Bassett.   'Come, let's talk sense.
You shall feed with me at the club, and
then I'll introduce you to the prettiest little
dancer——'

'Ralph Bassett, does your father know?'

'Don't be an ass, Lawrence.   "Does your
mother know you're out?" is a street question
that went out of date in London ages ago.
I'm sorry to think it survives in Bengal.
Come along.'

'Your father does not know everything
about his son; and yet you tell me that you
must needs know everything about your father.
Did he never hear the chimes at midnight, do
you suppose?   But, as you very sensibly say,
"come along," and, if he never did, with the
help of Shylock we will.'

He who, unlike Ralph Bassett, is able to
carry his memory about a generation back,
will be at some loss to identify the John
Doyle who had left so curious a reputation in
India, with that Jack Doyle who had once
represented the back-slums of Bohemian
London. For the hopeless, aimless, penniless,
shiftless sot to develop into a well-dressed,
sober, healthy, middle-aged gentleman, with
a reputation for too successful usury, was a
process of evolution, or rather revolution,
that seemed to require at least two eternities
and a meeting of the poles, with three or four
miracles thrown in. Had Charley Bassett's
son ever heard his father speak of Jack Doyle,
he could not have hesitated for a moment
before setting down his chance fellow-traveller
as the most flagrant of impostors. And yet
so unconscious are we of the changes which
take place in ourselves, however unnatural
and extravagant they may seem, that it was
the everyday commonplace development of
an amateur dilettante Bohemian into a baronet
and the father of a grown-up son that struck
John Doyle as really remarkable.

'And yet,' he thought to himself, as he
next morning set out to walk in a northerly

direction from his hotel in Covent Garden, 'I suppose I was fool enough in my heart to fancy I should find everything standing stock still. I wonder if I really believed that I should find Charley, and Esdaile, and Urquhart, and Ronaine, still gambling for millions in Gray's Inn Square? I believe that was what I expected to find. And so Esdaile and Ronaine may be on the other side of the earth, if they're not under it, and Urquhart is going to be a judge, and Charley Bassett is a rich baronet, with a son old enough to take up life at the point where I left the father. I wonder what makes me feel as if he'd changed in more than in that way? No; Charley Bassett wasn't the man to be silent about his friends. And never to have told the story of that child—the link that was to keep us all bound together, wherever we might be! Whatever has become of the others she ought to be flourishing, that girl, with one of her fathers making a fortune at the bar, and another with thousands a year. Why, my miserable allowance must have been a mere drop in the well. Ronaine's right, she ought to be the most accomplished young woman in London. I have it—by George!

Charley is keeping her dark out of fear for his son. Yes, if that young man came across any objectionable young woman, there might be the devil to pay before it was all done. Any man can be turned round any woman's thumb, of course; but that young fellow, to judge from his cut, could be turned round any schoolgirl's little finger. No; may be, if I were in his boat, I shouldn't care to introduce my son and heir to an accomplished young woman who had been picked up by chance in Gray's Inn Gardens, till she was safely married, anyhow, and may be not even then. . . . I wonder how other men feel, who've been spending a quarter of a life abroad, without making a friend, and come home again at last to find no hand to welcome them; not so much as an enemy's to be raised against them. . . . No, I don't. I wonder what men feel who come back to find welcome, and love, and home? My old garret and starvation were better than this sort of thing. And then they abuse me for being fond of money; as if one wouldn't be fond of the ugliest thing on earth if it was the only creature that stuck to one, and the only creature one had to live for. Aren't they fond of money themselves? But

then it isn't the one only thing to others that
it is to me.   Well, one woman has once done
one good thing.   She's sobered a sot, and
made a money-maker out of a madman.   I
suppose gold and water does make a whole-
somer drink than the other thing.   I'll make
enough to found a hospital for poor devils
who don't deserve helping, men who've come
to grief by their own faults and their own
follies—aren't faults and follies the biggest
misfortunes of all?   And I'll make myself the
first pensioner, and write a series of sermons
on the text about vanity. . . . Some broken-
down vagabond will be safe to stick to me
like a dog, so that I sha'n't go out of the
world without some sort of a shake of the
hand, though I daresay of a dirty one. . . .
Now, where am I going?   I'm hanged if it
isn't the old road to Gray's Inn ; as if I should
find a soul there !'

His conscious and coherent manner of
thinking argued the man who lives so much
alone as to have nobody but himself to talk
to.   The quarter could by rights have no
sort of sentimental charm for him ; and yet
he lingered.   The memory of a garret, in
defiance of right, has more than a sentimental

charm to the man who has once been driven
to live in one, at least so soon as he is driven
to live in one no longer. The very smell of
Holborn recalled hundreds of hideous memories, and yet with something of the pathetic
suggestiveness of stocks and wall-flowers upon
sensitive nerves.

'I'll look in a Law List and look up
Urquhart,' said he. 'He'll be somewhere in
the Temple, I suppose. From what I heard
in the train, we're like to have the sympathy
of twin gold grubbers, he and I. And I shall
hear how the land lies with Charley; and I
may as well hear how that child's turned out
after all, though she is a girl. I am glad
she's got a baronet for one father and a
coming judge for another. That hospital for
undeserving incapables will get twenty pounds
a year more. I wish I'd known sooner. Let
me see, twenty pounds a year and interest; I
might have saved nearly five hundred pounds,
instead of, at my time of life, throwing it
away on a girl; a fine lady, no doubt, who
spends five pounds a quarter on gloves and
ribbons. However, I mustn't complain,' he
thought, with a sigh. 'I should never have
made my first five-pound note but for her.

Whatever I am now, I'm what she's made me.
Yes ; I'll look up Urquhart.   May be Esdaile
or Ronaine may turn out good subjects for
that hospital, especially Ronaine.   I wonder
if they've found it as hard to keep up their
twenty pounds a year as I used to do; or if
the fight has ended with them as it has with
me ? '

# CHAPTER V

### THE FATE OF PHILOSOPHY

AT the end of the very few minutes which carry one from Holborn to the Temple, Doyle (to call him Jack any longer is henceforth out of the question) had discovered the business chambers of Mr. Urquhart in Elm Court, and had knocked at the door. But, to his disappointment, he learned that Mr. Urquhart was not at chambers that day ; that he was going out of town to attend some arbitration in the North, but that he would be found at home up to three in the afternoon by anybody who wished to see him urgently. Now, what can possibly be more urgent than the welcome of an old friend who has just come home from India after an absence of many years ? So Doyle, feeling in himself an increasingly urgent need of the long-forgotten luxury of the touch of the hand of a friend, and having nothing more profitable to do, made a short calculation of the time it would take him to get from the Temple to Fonthill Gardens, Hyde Park, and stopped the first omnibus that would take him in that direction. Not even the claims and desires of old friendship seemed more urgent than the duty of saving so unprofitable an investment as a cab-fare.

It seemed odd to him that so distinguished a member of the brotherhood of the close fist, to which Urquhart, unlike the converted archdeacon, had belonged from the beginning, should have a house as well as his chambers. Urquhart had been the man, even in the good old times, to dispense, not only with cheap comforts—they all, even Charley Bassett, did that—but with such much more essential things as extravagant luxuries. It seemed even odder when Fonthill Gardens (which he had some difficulty in finding, seeing that Hyde Park meant a remote corner of Paddington) turned out to be one of those obtrusively new No Thoroughfares, which look entirely given over to the very height or depth of respectable domesticity. He was utterly unfamiliar with this aspect of semi-suburban London, and, under the influence of the universal expectation that everything else must stand still, while we ourselves move on from change to change, half wondered whether Mr. Urquhart, of the Temple and Fonthill Gardens, could possibly be the same as the ancient philosopher of Gray's Inn.

A barrel-organ—the only familiar sight or sound in the place—suddenly broke out into an imperfect and disjointed version of 'Cari luoghi, vi ravviso.' Jack Doyle, of Bohemia, had had an ear for tunes; Mr. Doyle, from Bengal, had a memory for them. And this particular stop of the crazy organ struck him as a very bad joke indeed. He did not throw the grinder a penny as he knocked at Mr. Urquhart's door. For the sake of the badness of the joke, the old Jack Doyle would have thrown him two, if he had them. But times were changed.

They were changed indeed. The door of Number Eighteen was thrown open by a man-servant in livery.

'Does Mr. Urquhart live here?' asked Doyle. 'Is he at home?'

'Mrs. Urquhart is at home,' said the footman.

Mrs. Urquhart! Then the last possible change had come ; the experimental philoso-

pher had committed himself to the only experiment which he had held too irrevocable
to be made.

Doyle smiled sadly, and sighed grimly.
This, then, accounted for the house in Fonthill
Gardens, and the footman.

' Mr. Urquhart is out of town,' said the
latter. ' He is not expected back for some
days.'

' I will see Mrs. Urquhart,' said Doyle,
giving his card. ' I must see the woman who
was too much for his philosophy,' thought he.
But he felt, ' I must know something of my
old friends. I must find out if anything is
left that isn't changed.'

The house, he noticed as he went upstairs
into the drawing-room, was expensively and
even ambitiously furnished, and yet felt
wanting in that first duty of every house
towards all who enter its door—the sense of
hospitality. Nobody can guess how, or why,
or whence it comes ; few consciously note its
absence ; but nothing on earth is felt more
quickly or keenly, whether in relation to a
palace or a hovel. He entered the drawing-
room in anything but the humour for making
a first call on a strange lady. He was dis-

appointed at not having found Urquhart, and at having found his friend's life so altered. He was anything but a lady's-man, and was already repenting of the impulse of curiosity which had led him into his present situation. A piece of furniture out of place, or a symptom of litter, would have proved a connecting link between the old times and the new. But there was nothing of the kind.

'When Mrs. Urquhart asks me to stay here,' he thought to himself, 'I think I'll say —no.'

He had waited full ten minutes when Mrs. Urquhart came into the room. Of course she was not what he had expected to see; as little like a subject for psychological experiments as can well be imagined. She was tall, with a great many more angles than curves; not ill-featured, but with no signs, in her middle age, of having been married for her beauty. Doyle's eyes, indifferent to the details of any woman's looks, passed over her length of nose, bad complexion, and too pronounced redness of hair, but they did not pass over a sour expression that one does not look for in a presumably happy wife and mother.

'The experiment hasn't the look of having

turned out well,' thought he. But then he
had always, on principle, looked in marriage
for the wrong things.

'Mr. Doyle?' asked Mrs. Urquhart, not
at all ungraciously, but still with a little
more of the stiff doubtfulness which, however
prudent towards a stranger, is inconsistent
with the hope of an early thaw. 'I am sorry
to say Mr. Urquhart is from home, but if it is
on business——'

'I'm sorry for that. I must introduce
myself, then. I am an old friend of Urquhart;
I came back from India only yesterday, and
he is the first man in London I've called on.
I didn't know there was a Mrs. Urquhart till
I knocked at the door. Is it too late to congratulate him on—on—on—such a change?'

Mrs. Urquhart did not seem to be impressed by seeing for the first time an old
friend of her husband's bachelor days.

'I've no doubt Mr. Urquhart will be very
sorry when he hears you've called,' she said;
'but he is so busy, and I really don't know
when he'll be home.'

What Doyle, professing contempt if not
downright dislike for the sex, had expected
from a strange woman, he could hardly have

told ; but he had certainly not expected the chilling silence that Mrs. Urquhart allowed to follow her precisely measured phrases.  It was almost as much as if she had said, in so many words : 'I take no interest in my husband's bachelor friends, and I don't want to know them, and I don't want him to have anything more to do with them.'  But a man's bachelor friends are notoriously slow to read such signs, and Doyle only felt the chill without catching the tolerably obvious cause.  And, at any rate, he could hardly take up his hat and leave the room without making some show of talk for at least the formal quarter of an hour. So much manners, at least, he had learned in Bengal, if, indeed, they were not a relic of some otherwise long-forgotten existence previous to his knowledge of Urquhart, Bassett, Esdaile, and Ronaine.  For he must have come from somewhere ; no man was ever born a Jack Doyle.

'Urquhart seems to have been carrying everything before him since we lost sight of one another,' said he.  'I hear him talked of for the Bench, and I see that he ought to be the happiest man in the world.'

Jack Doyle had never been famous for

compliments to man or woman, but he was
rewarded for this by what might pass for a
wintry smile.

'I suppose you've often heard of those
rough old times when he was eating his way
through the Middle Temple. They were
rough days; but——well, nobody is ever
sorry for having known them. Urquhart and
I must make a pilgrimage to the old places,
and see how we feel in them now—if they're
not changed too.'

'Yes, Mr. Doyle,' said Mrs. Urquhart,
with a sharp little emphasis, 'things do
change, and a good thing too.'

'H'm—that depends. However, Urquhart's all right of course? In health I
mean? Of course he always used to keep
his head cool. I think I was the only man
he could never manage to see under the
table, but I daresay he could do that now.
In India, Mrs. Urquhart, one gets out of
training, you see.'

'Pardon me,' said Mrs. Urquhart, 'if I
do not quite understand what you mean.'

'Ah, am I telling tales out of school?
Then you must pardon me. Urquhart was
always our good boy.'

'I am quite sure,' said the lady, 'that Mr. Urquhart never did anything that he would not wish me to know.'

'Oh, of course. Well, anyhow, here he is, a great lawyer, and a married man, and I don't know what besides.—I can't stand more of this,' thought he, by way of filling up the fresh spell of silence. 'I see how it is; Urquhart has been trying the experiment of marrying a woman with money, and for money, and for nothing else, I should say. So—well, there's an end of him.—I'm afraid, Mrs. Urquhart, I must be going now. But I mustn't forget to ask after our daughter, though I'm afraid I must plead guilty to having forgotten half her names. I hope she has not quite turned out the prodigy that some of us meant her to be?'

'"Our daughter," Mr. Doyle? I said Mr. Urquhart tells me everything, of course. But he can hardly be expected to remember every joke that he ever heard made. Of course I'm very sorry if you must go, but if you must——'

'I mean the child that we named Jane Burden. I remember my own share in her christening, though I'm vague about the rest. Let me see ; she was to be a Psyche to Urquhart, I believe, to represent an unformed soul——Poor fellow!' he thought to himself again, 'fancy being tied to a woman who can't understand one word without the help of twenty; I hope she was worth marrying; but if she were worth the Bank of England, and only cost sixpence, she'd be sixpence too dear.'

He thought the lady suddenly looked exceedingly grave and strange. She drew herself up stiffly, glanced at the bell-handle, and then looked him full in the face, as she said, in a tone as clear, and as sharp, and as cold as the edge of an icicle :

'I cannot possibly be expected to know who you are, except that your card tells me your name is Doyle, and that you pro-fess to have known Mr. Urquhart when— when he did not know me. Why anybody should have come all the way from India to insult me to my own face, I really do not know. So I will tell you at once that you will find it no use—no use at all. I know everything, Mr. Doyle.'

'Is the woman crazy ?' thought he.

'Yes, to insult me to my very face,' she went on, without a change of tone. Perhaps—though you mayn't think it—I know more of you than you suppose. I have heard of you, Mr. Doyle, though, of course, I did not care to say so when you called. Indeed, I did not identify you at first. There are a good many people named Doyle ; but I know now, and I am glad I, and not Mr. Urquhart, was at home. I need not tell you of his weakness—how foolishly ready he is to throw away money upon everybody who has ever known him well enough to bow to him. I am a very different sort of person, Mr. Doyle.'

'Mad as a March hare!' was the only thought that could come to him. 'The woman who can accuse Urquhart of throwing away a single sixpence must be ripe for Bedlam. Poor fellow!' he added, more than half aloud.

'Understand, once for all,' said she, 'that I don't know whether that—that child is named Jane or Sukey, or anything else, and that I don't care. If you want to profit by any trumped-up story of my husband's past life, I can only say you

have come to the wrong person. When I
discovered—never mind how—that Mr.
Urquhart was privately paying money to
some washerwoman or other for the maintenance of a child, you may be sure I was
sensible enough to ask him plainly what he
meant by such a thing. He was weak enough
to tell me some impossible story of a nursery-
maid and a foundling, which, I need not say,
I did not believe. He had to own to the
truth at last, for understand that my property
is settled on myself, and that I may do with
it just what I please—income and all. He
had to own that the child was not his—for,
of course, if it had been, I could not have
forgiven him—but that he was charitably
helping to keep the deserted infant of some
disreputable acquaintance. No wonder he
had tried to keep me in the dark about such
a foolish piece of folly! And he had to confess at last that the name of that child's father
was—Doyle. I won't repeat the things I
made him tell me about that man. I won't
suppose that you are that man, though you
have the same name. But, if you think I
have allowed Mr. Urquhart to continue aid-
ing and abetting the immoral conduct of other

people, all I can tell you is, that the child
may be dead for anything I and Mr. Urquhart
know. And the best thing, too—poor, miserable, deserted, neglected little thing!'

She rose and moved towards the bell.

Doyle rose also. Mrs. Urquhart certainly
did not seem in the least afraid of him, and he
gave her no cause. His slight approach to
her was heavy and slow, and though his
voice deepened, it was certainly not with
anger. She was not likely to notice how the
bronze of his face deepened also.

'I forgot that, being a woman, you must
needs have a woman's heart,' said he. 'As
to Urquhart—well, I suppose that married
men are bound to get into corners now and
then, and must get out as best they can. . .
And what's the use of having an absent friend
if one can't use his shoulders? Make yourself
easy, Mrs. Urquhart. You say you don't
like to tell me what—Mr. Urquhart said of
Jack Doyle. I'll tell you, and you shall tell
me if I'm wrong. He called me a shiftless,
drunken, disreputable sot, living on brandy
that other people were fools enough to pay
for—an animal, or beast, rather, wallowing in
the dregs of other people's vices—a man whom

he was ashamed of having known, half blackguard, half fool——'

'He never called you a fool, Mr. Doyle,'
said she politely.

Never did quarrel come off with less show
of anger on either side.

'Then I may take it he did call me all
the rest—and every word of it was true ; and
as he did not add fool, I do.   And now listen
to me.   I will drag no man's name but my
own through the mire, since a woman and
a wife, and may be a mother, thinks it mire
to be found out in helping a helpless baby
not to starve.   Don't be afraid.   I'm not
angry with your husband for speaking of
me as he found me.   I won't trouble his
domestic happiness by reminding him that
he once upon a time—before he knew you
—knew a blackguard named Jack Doyle.
I'll only find out who else has broken the
bond that I have kept, and that was to
hold six men together against the world,
wherever we might be.   And then——'

'Yes, Mr. Doyle?'

'Then I shall think better of women,
because I shall have to think worse of men.
I have been a believer in my own sex,

though not in yours. And so, good-morning.
You need not even tell Mr. Urquhart I have
called, unless you please.'

'Then—excuse my anxiety—I may understand that the child is yours ?'

'It seems to be nobody else's, anyhow,'
said he, with the nearest approach to heat he
had shown.

He could not, before he left the house, tell
Mrs. Urquhart, because he had never yet
told himself, the story of how he had become
changed. But, as he strode away in no particular direction from Fonthill Gardens, and
thought of how Urquhart had thrown over so
slight and cheap a trust to save himself from
the suspicions of a jealous woman, he began
to suspect Bassett's silence to his son concerning so innocent a story, and to be angry with
himself for quite another sort of folly. Had
that bond in Gray's Inn Square been a mere
farce to fill up an idle hour ? He had never
even pretended to care a straw about the fate
of the child ; and he could not look back
upon his first struggle to fulfil his share of
the bond without horror. It was not for the
child's, but for his more than half-drunken
word's sake, that he had forced himself,

against the hopeless lethargy of mind and
body which had become second nature to
him, to earn the first instalment of five pounds
to be paid into Mrs. Nelson's hands. He
remembered still how Charley Bassett had
stared when he roughly refused the latter's
offer to undertake his share of the burden,
saying, only in less decent language, 'No;
when five wise men get tricked by one woman,
big or little, five fools must pay.' He did not
remember clearly the way in which he had,
somehow or other, ground out that first
five pounds. The memory was hopelessly
obscured by the big drink which had followed
an extraordinary spell of desperate sobriety.
But another five pounds had to be got in
another quarter; and so, to the sincere
though unconfessed relief of all who knew him,
he turned over on his side and rolled out of
his London garret into the office of some
newspaper in India, where, it was fondly
hoped, he might speedily be buried under the
influence of brandy without pawnee. 'Poor
Jack,' was his spoken epitaph: 'He was a
good fellow, but——' And at 'but' all that
could be said of him aloud came to an end.
He seemed to have exhausted himself in the

feat of working for, and earning, five pounds, without drinking it in sixpences by the way. Jack drunk had been getting bad enough, but Jack sober was not to be borne. He showed, in this condition, too many signs of what the ultra-Bohemian comes to be, when, as sometimes happens, he grows old. So, as it seemed, he went out of sight and under water, and was missed for nine not unpleasant days. His friends lamented him warmly ; but how many mourners would be overjoyed if a friend whom they buried yesterday were to walk in at the door to-day ? He would, at any rate, have the bad taste to put everything out, and.to throw discredit on his own funeral. Nobody (and he knew it) cared twopence about the end of Jack Doyle.

How it was that the chance nickname of Archdeacon had followed him out to India, the few, if any there be, who understand such things must explain. It seems likely enough that a nickname, once given, becomes part of a man, from which he cannot be freed without being flayed. No man with a nickname would be surprised to hear himself greeted by it on a first introduction to some strange mandarin in the heart of China. But it no longer bore the old meaning ; indeed, it came to have no discoverable meaning at all. That first fight for five pounds had left its traces upon him ; and, little by little, as time dragged on, the same recurring need became a sort of Fetish—a third nature which gained ground upon the second. Nor could he, after a while, make five pounds without making a good many more. And, unknown to himself, that invisible bond was closely hugged as the only sort of chain that bound him to another living soul.

'And it was a farce,' thought he, 'if I am the only one to whom it has been more than a straw. There is Esdaile, and there is Ronaine ; but where are they? That young fellow had never heard their names. I may be wronging Bassett—and I know nothing of the others ; and so there's only one thing for it. And that is, here goes.'

Honestly, he would have given a good deal of money, say five shillings, to avoid seeing the girl who had forced him out of Bohemia against his will, and changed him into whatever he was now. But his heart had been growing sore as well as hungry. His business in England was to see his old friends, half thinking to find them as of old, as the one makeshift open to him for home. And he had found one a baronet, and another a henpecked lawyer; what would the others prove?

'As poor as Job, and much less married, I hope with all my heart,' he thought as he went, at last, towards Gray's Inn. His quarterly remittance had bound him to know that Mr. Nelson's official address was still with Messrs. Mark and Simple. That, at least, had never changed. And, considering all the circumstances, the continuance of the admiral in the same situation for so many years was considerably more remarkable than the change of an amateur Bohemian into a county magnate, of a Jack Doyle into a reputed miser, or even of a Philosopher into the husband of a jealous shrew. For, after all, all these things have been known before, from the days of Socrates downwards.

Doyle had not been in Gray's Inn Square since the night when Marion Eve Pysche Zenobia Dulcibella Jane received her names. And he thought it strange that the hand of a man who had long forsworn brandy should tremble a little as it knocked on that same old door of green baize.

## CHAPTER VI

### A SUDDEN LEAP

FOR some days after Phil Nelson's adventure
with the guitar, Phœbe's garden walks were
uninterrupted. Stanislas Adrianski had van-
ished, and had left a sense of emptiness in his
place which she had never known before.
The withered laurel-bush, once so suggestive
of boundless forests, had become but a
withered laurel-bush not only in fact but in
seeming, and sunset upon the snow-covered
mountains was reduced to the falling of blacks
upon a prospect of damp linen. Even Phil
had taken himself off to distant countries with
a 'Good-bye' so cold and short that it had
almost made her angry ; and his absence made
her miss her romance-hero all the more. She
had known nothing of the serenade ; for, just
as if she had been the most sensible of girls,
sentiment with her never disturbed sleep, and

she had only heard of it next morning as a drunken street row—a belief which neither Phil nor Dick, for different reasons, cared to overturn.

So Phil had gone, and her hero had disappeared, and she had nothing to do but to make up her mind that life, real life, was a sadly empty and unsatisfactory condition of things. She had absolutely nothing else to do, for domestic affairs in that household were matters of minutes, and, these over, she had the rest of the day upon her hands. She could not help thinking of Stanislas, if only by way of filling up her time. Now she thought he had fallen ill; and, if so, what was the duty of a heroine towards a hero and a patriot, sick and friendless in a foreign land? Alas! the duty, considered from a romantic point of view, was so inconveniently clear, that she gave that guess up as not to be thought of. No; he could not be ill, because that would oblige her to go and nurse him— a duty which presented such a formidable list of difficulties that she gave up conquering them even in fancy before she was half-way through. Besides, the fact of a neighbour's illness would have found its way through the party-walls, which, in their street, had tongues as well as ears. Had Phil's savage rudeness offended him ? But surely a nobleman would not condescend to notice the insults of a sullen boor. Or—could it be, could it possibly be, that the patriot feared for the heart that should be his country's alone?

Such thoughts, if thoughts they can be called, do not grow weaker in solitude. She not only thought a great deal of Stanislas Adrianski, but also of the Associated Robespierres, and of the mystery of her own life ; and she thought that she was thinking hard. In spite of her instincts in that direction, nature had not yet taught her to be enough of a coquette to keep resolutely indoors, so that she might learn from a corner of the window if her absence had the power to draw Stanislas into his back garden. She would learn maidenly cunning soon enough, no doubt; but, meanwhile, she behaved with a simplicity that will be called either straightforward, or only forward, according to varying views. She could not walk up and down stairs all day for exercise, or look out of the front windows all day long for pastime, so she made herself look as nice as she could, and

took a book out into the garden. And that
book was 'Thaddeus of Warsaw.'

But it was in vain. And it was with real
vexation and disappointment, as if somebody
had failed to keep tryst, that, after reading
three pages at the rate of a page an hour,
she went indoors again. She had expected
nothing definite when she went out, but felt,
none the less, that life was using her badly.
That was the day on the morning of which
Phil, at desperately short notice, had started
for Russia; and her present mood made her
wish him at home. She wanted to quarrel
with somebody about something, and Phil
would have done better to quarrel with than
anybody she knew. Altogether, she was very
lonesome and very dull; so much so, that by
the close of another empty day she began to
feel quite superior to the rest of the world, on
the score of her capacity for being lonely and
dull. She sought food for lofty scorn from
the vulgar high spirits of the boys, and found
what she sought, and listened to her father's
eloquence without being able to screw herself
up to the proper pitch of enthusiasm for a
cause that, in the person of Stanislas, had
once more become invisible to her. 'Revolu-

tions aren't made with rosewater,' he had quoted to her, with his fiercest voice, over his sixth cup of tea. 'No; I suppose rosewater would not go well with whisky,' she had answered, without a thought of sarcasm, and with a real sigh. She felt like growing old before her time, and getting behind the scenes.

The next day she did not feel it worth while to take any particular pains to make herself look nice; she rather underdid her toilette, if anything. The garden looked so empty and ugly that she did not care to go there, and 'Thaddeus of Warsaw' had grown as stupid as a book could be. It was honestly without the least expectation of seeing anybody that she went out at last; just as one must when there is the barest apology for a garden, and when one is tired of being alone indoors. So her heart gave an honest leap when she heard over the wall and behind her:

'Good-morning, mademoiselle.'

Stanislas Adrianski's voice was always soft, and his accent always, even when talking about himself—perhaps especially then— caressing and tender. But it was in the

coldest of tones, a tone so cold as to surprise
herself, that she answered him, shortly:

' Good-morning.'

There was absolutely no reason for her
even pretending to be cold, and she was not
pretending. And yet she felt her heart
fluttering all the while. She turned round,
and, in a moment her coldness left her.
Stanislas Adrianski looked very pale, and
more melancholy than ever—and no wonder,
for he wore a long strip of plaister from the
middle of his forehead to his left cheek-bone,
crossed by another strip above the eye.

' Oh, what has happened? You have been
ill!' she cried.

' But it is nothing,' said he. 'Nothing at
all. I have been wounded worse as that,
twenty, thirty, forty times. I am glad—the
sun shines from your garden into mine, and I
forget the pain.'

' But what has happened? Is it the
Czar?'

' No, not the Czar. Never mind. I
should not have shown myself, but I saw
you, and——'

He did not finish his sentence, and she
was not much attending to his words, full of

romantic promise as they were. She was wishing that she had made herself look her nicest
to-day instead of yesterday. She was thinking
how it always happens that when one looks
for something nothing happens, and that
something only happens when one expects
nothing. And she might have asked herself
how far she was answerable for a meeting that
she had courted, though it had come without
courting. She did not object to the effect of
the plaister, nor, though it looked comical
enough to common eyes, did it look so to
hers. She did not think that the count looked
like a fiddler who had been fighting at a fair.
Why should a broken head be less interesting
than a sprained ankle in a woman or a broken
arm in a man?

'But you have been wounded——' she
began.

'I tell you it is nothing. I do not make
brags, mademoiselle. Only, when one insults
a lady before a gentleman, what can I do?
In my country we do not speech, we blow.'

'Blow? Ah, I see; but who——'

'Pardon, mademoiselle. What I have
done, I have done; but what I have done,
nothing shall make me tell—no, not even

you. We will speak of other things. I hope you are quite well.'

She thought for a moment. Then a glorious hope came to her—for is it not glory to be fought about by two brave men? If Phœbe had been told that Helen of Troy was ashamed of the fuss made over her, she would not have believed.

'Oh, please, pray tell me,' she said eagerly, laying both her hands upon the wall, while her cheeks glowed; 'pray tell me you have not been quarrelling with Phil!'

He removed his cigarette, bowed down, and put his lips to her nearest hand. The kiss felt like a little sting, and she snatched her hand away, looking round to be sure that Mrs. Goodge or any of the neighbours had not seen. It was the first time such a thing had happened to her, and it frightened her, while it made her proud.

'A patriot and a soldier does not lie,' said he. 'I did not mean to say my secret. But, as you surprise him, I cannot deny. I hear to-day he is gone—that young man. He will trouble you no more.'

It did not strike her, even as a coincidence, that Stanislas Adrianski's first re-

appearance was on the day of his hearing
that Phil Nelson had gone away. She was
simply thinking that he was indeed a noble
gentleman.

'And Phil said nothing about it,' said she.
'I am very angry with both of you—very
angry indeed. Are you very much hurt?
And—how was it that Phil didn't seem hurt
at all?'

'If you are angry,' said Stanislas, 'I am
miserable: the most miserable in the world.
He did not seem hurt—no? Because he
attacked me like a man in fury. I challenged
him, I mean to say; but before I could cry
"En garde," on he came, and with his weapon
struck me where you see. Well, mademoiselle, if you will look, you will find him
all over blue and black—under his clothes.
I must speak the truth, since I speak something at all. I challenge, but I do not hurt
the face—no. That is for cowards; and
in my country we are brave. You must
not be angry, mademoiselle.'

'You beat Phil? Why, he is as strong and
as brave as a lion! I didn't think there was
a man who could beat Phil.'

For a moment Stanislas Adrianski did not

look quite so amiably melancholy as usual. But it was only for a moment.

'For any good cause I would do as much as that,' said he, 'and for your sake I would do more. For your sake I would beat him ten times.'

'Once is too often,' she said. 'Promise me——'

'Pardon! I promise what else you will. But not to fight a man who insults you— no.'

'You must be very strong and very brave. How is it your country is conquered, if all the Poles are like you?'

'Ah, mademoiselle, but they are not all like me. If they were—— But I am glad they are not, because then I should not be here.'

Phœbe wanted to say something, but could think of nothing to please her. How was it that he was so ready with everything that a man ought to say? She could not, somehow, manage to think that, were Phil's skin examined, it would be found so very black or blue. But that was all the better; for, as she would scarcely have liked to think of him as being seriously damaged, she was thus able to imagine what she liked without any compunction.

'Mademoiselle,' said Stanislas, after a short but impressive silence, 'you know me what I seem to be. You do not know what I am. It is not the first time I challenge a man who insults a lady. But that time I did not beat with a stick. I killed him with the sword.'

Phœbe started, and almost gave a little scream. It was grand and beautiful, but it was also terrible.

'You—you have killed a man?'

'I am a soldier, mademoiselle. A soldier must kill.'

'Oh, in battle of course, but——. Is she very beautiful?'

'She?'

'Didn't you say it was for a—a lady you —you killed that man?'

'Did I say that? But—I did not mean to say my secret. But, as you surprise him, I cannot deny. She was beautiful—— But, on the faith of a patriot, she is nothing to me—nothing at all. We will speak of other things. The poor Natalie! But she is nothing to you.'

This was a little more than Phœbe had

bargained for, and her curiosity about this new element of romance was almost more than she could restrain. To talk to a man who had killed another man for a woman's sake was better than reading 'Thaddeus of Warsaw' for the first time. She almost felt jealous that Phil had escaped with only a drubbing. She would not have wished any-thing worse, of course ; but it lowered her own little romance before Natalie's great one.

'It does interest me very much,' she said gently. 'How unhappy she must be !'

'Why ? '

'To think of you, who did all that for her sake, in exile, and——'

'Oh, no. After all, they console them-selves, those women, for what we risk our honour and our lives. She loved me well. But not so well, when my country called me away, to say, "Go." I loved her very pretty well, too, but not so well as Poland—no. And so she consoles herself, and I love her no more. She is grand dame. I am the poor exile. And that is all.'

'Why did you call her " poor " ? '

'Because she is rich, mademoiselle. Be-

cause she chose gold, and grandeur, and all
such things, before me.'

Phœbe was touched in a very weak point
indeed.

'I would have said, " Go " ! ' she said, not
only out of her fancy, but out of her heart ;
'and if you had not gone, I would never
have spoken to you again ! '

She was certainly a girl with the most
chaotic of brains, supposing her to keep such
things.   Even as she spoke the words, she
was pleased with them as the echo of something out of some half-remembered story-
book ; she meant them to be effective, and
yet she felt them and meant them, not thinking of how much farther they might be taken,
in all simple sincerity and zeal.   If she believed in shams, and in nothing else, she
believed as much as  she  knew how, and
never stopped halfway.   To her confusion,
Stanislas, without dropping his cigarette from
his lips, placed his hands upon the low wall,
and vaulted over to her side with much grace,
if little dignity.

'I know it ! ' he said.   'You would say,
" Go," and you would make it death to go !
I thank you, mademoiselle.   I believe in

woman once more. You wake a dead heart out of the grave.'

It was indeed lucky that Phil had gone. Though he must needs be miles away, Phœbe could not help looking round for a moment out of an habitual fear of a presence that she now knew she had always feared. Stanislas took one of her hands, and smiled down upon her with an air of defiant protection.

'No,' he said, 'I am an exile. I am alone. I am friendless. I am poor. I have only my sword, and my name—Stanislas Adrianski, nothing more. But if you were the Queen of England, I would not be afraid. You would not say, " Go away; I am, perhaps, great lady. I show you the door." You will only ask, " Is Adrianski a patriot? Is Adrianski brave? Does Adrianski love?" And you will say, " Yes. Adrianski is a patriot; Adrianski is brave; Adrianski loves;" for it is true, mademoiselle. I leap over the wall because you are the angel of my dream. You are the queen of the soul of Adrianski. Ah, what I suffer for you! If you have not pity—ah, what death ! ah, what despair ! '

This was another sort of wooing, indeed, from poor Phil's.

He was now holding both her hands, with
the tender strength that is not to be denied,
and her eyes were held and fascinated by
the light and fire that glowed and deepened
in Adrianski's. Did she love him? She no
more knew that than she knew Stanislas
Adrianski. But one thing she did know—
that Phœbe Burden, not to speak of the
adopted daughter of the Grand President of
the Associated Robespierres, and a possible
duchess in her own right, could not tell a
poor, homeless, friendless, noble patriot hero
to leap back over the wall from the garden of
hope into that of despair without a more
than commonly kind word. Had he been a
Czar, romance itself would have compelled
her to say, Go. But how could she do what
Natalie had done? Where Natalie had said,
Stay, Phœbe must say, Go. Where Natalie
would have said, Go, was not Phœbe compelled to say, or at least to look, Stay?

It was rather a yellow afternoon, bad for
health, but fairly safe for sentiment, seeing
that the neighbours were not likely to be
looking out of their back windows.

'Ah,' said Stanislas, looking down into
her eyes with a less glowing but more tender

gaze, 'when you know who you are—well, you will be like the rest of them; all I have ever—heard of. You will forget; and you will be consoled.'

He was taking possession of her, it seemed, without doubt or question. Had Phœbe given herself and her life into the keeping of Stanislas Adrianski? She could not tell for certain; but the situation itself was claiming her. Supposing that she had given herself to him, then the charge that she, Phœbe, would or could forget and throw over a man because she turned out to be rich and great, while he remained poor, was too outrageous to be borne.

'Never!' she exclaimed, speaking half for herself, the true Phœbe, but at least half for that heroine with whom, at last, and after years of waiting, she had become fully and fairly one. 'How could I—how could any woman do that—how could she do it; that other girl, I mean, who gave you up because you were unhappy; because you were so brave? The greater I was, and the poorer and more unhappy anybody was——'

'The more you would stoop and raise him up? I know; you have a soul made of diamonds and pearls.  You may be a princess, and you accept the heart and the lyre and the sword of the poor patriot, the poor exile. I am in heaven, mademoiselle.  Ah, but I fear ! '

It was too late to ask herself if she loved him now.  She knew something at last—that, whatever might happen to-morrow, she had to-day fallen into a net from which she could not escape without treason to her views of life, and a sense of being as unworthy as Natalie.  Not that she wanted to escape ; but it was rather sudden, this conquest by storm, and she wished this invincible hero had allowed her a little while to think everything out, and say Yes out of a little more freedom of will.  And yet it was a proud thing to have love made to her by a real hero, in the real heroic, unquestioning, all-conquering style.  It gave her no time to think, and thinking would have meant having to face all sorts of mean and paltry difficulties in detail from which she had been saved.  In short, Stanislas Adrianski was as clearly her fate as if she had read it in large letters in the sky.  Right or wrong, for good or ill, it was a glory to spend an hour in having secret and

passionate love made to her by a man like
this, who had now acquired, in addition to his
other attractions, the fascination of being
terrible. For had he not proved that he
knew how to love, not only with the heart
but with the sword? He had said, 'But I
fear.' What could 'fear' mean to such a
man as he?

'Ah, but I fear,' he said again. 'Say it
is pride, say it is jealousy, say it is what you
will. How can I tell this will not be a dream,
that I shall wake to-morrow and find you
have opened your wings and fled all away?
I, Adrianski, am afraid. Say, whatever
happens, whatever comes to you, you will be
true as I. You will be a princess, near to a
queen, when Poland is free. But one may
wait, and wait, and ah, meanwhile! Say,
whatever happens, whatever comes, you will
be true. Oh, mademoiselle! do not again
throw me into despair! Hold my hand, and
say, "Stanislas, my friend, whatever comes,
whatever happens, I will be true; I will be
your wife, and of no other man."'

For such absolute, downright committal
as this she was certainly unprepared. In her
heart she would have preferred an exciting

chapter of vague feelings, secret meetings,
unfettered castle-buildings, ending in something or nothing, whichever the pleasantest
end might be. This pledge sounded rather
solemn—a distinct pledge to a real man, who
had already shown himself her master.

'Oh, don't ask me to say that now,' she
stammered, beginning to be really afraid of
him. 'It is late, and I must go in——'

'Now or never!' said he. 'To-morrow!
It may never come.'

'Oh yes it will. And there——Hark!'
She started, for she heard, even in the
garden, the sound of a knock at the street-
door, so long and so loud as to make it
probable that it was the second or third time
of knocking. 'Oh, please let me go now—I
must go. Somebody is at the door—father,
most likely, or one of the boys, and if——'

For answer he clasped both her hands
more tightly. 'Now or never! I go not
back till you say, till you swear. Your
father and your brothers may come. What
do I mind?'

It was true they could not come without
breaking down the door. But she was really
frightened now.

'What am I to say?'

'Say—whatever happens, whatever comes, I will be the wife of Stanislas Adrianski, and of no other man.'

Again came the knock, louder than before.

'I say it—there,' she said, as she felt herself kissed quickly on both hands, on her forehead, and on her eyes. She saved her lips, and escaped into the house, while Stanislas, even more quickly, vaulted back over the wall.

# CHAPTER VII

### PHŒBE'S PICTURE

WHEN the door was at last opened, John Doyle (for it was he) saw before him a girl, woefully ill-dressed, and looking, in her fright and confusion, as if she had just been startled out of a sound sleep, or had been interrupted in the middle of a piece of mischief. He had looked for nothing less than to be met on the threshold by the very girl about whom he had come to inquire, and he had formed an idea of her very different, as a matter of course, from the reality presented to him by Phœbe.

'Does Mr. Nelson live here?' he asked, 'and is he at home?'

He did not put his question very courteously, for his temper, already tried by Mrs. Urquhart, had not been improved by having to knock three times at a door which he had intended, on coming to London, to avoid. It

was not in the child that he was interested,
but in the behaviour of his friends.

'Yes—no,' said Phœbe; 'I mean he does
live here, but he isn't at home.'

'Will he be in soon?'

'I expect him every minute.'

'Then I will come in and wait for him.
It is on business, and I shall not be able to
call again.'

It was an extraordinary thing that any
person, other than a collector of debts and rates
in arrear, should wish to see Mr. Nelson on
any sort of business any more than for pleasure,
and Phœbe felt that she saw before her an
Associated Robespierre. He far more nearly
came up to her ideal of such a character than
her father or any of her so-called father's so-
called friends, with his height, his breadth of
chest and shoulders, his deep, slow, heavy
voice, his bronzed complexion, and big beard.
Perhaps he might be the chief of all the Associated Robespierres all over the world; for
even in her present excitement she could not
leave unused the smallest loophole for a flight
of dramatic fancy.

The world had become full enough of
colour at last; almost too full for one time.

What with love and mystery, she felt plunged at once into the second volume of a novel without having read the first.

'Pray come in,' she said, and wished she had had the presence of mind to say 'Pray enter'—obviously a more appropriate phrase.

He followed her into the parlour, where it suddenly struck her that she had clean forgotten to lay out tea.

The room was now dark, as well as in a general muddle. It was always more or less the last, for what can one unpractical girl do against a host of impracticable boys?

So he waited at the door while she tried to turn on the gas—and failed. No hiss followed her attempt; and, when she struck a match, the air from the pipe blew it out, and left everything as dark as before.

'Perhaps it isn't turned on at the meter,' suggested her visitor.

'I'm afraid,' she said, 'it must be one of their days for cutting off the gas; they do, every now and then, two or three times a year. It's very tiresome. I'm afraid you must wait while I run out for some candles. It's only just round the corner. I sha'n't be a minute gone.'

She ran upstairs for her hat, and Doyle, finding his way to a horsehair sofa, sat down upon a pair of boots.

He gave up the idea of sitting down, and walked to the window, whence nothing but fog was now to be seen.

The girl had been gone rather longer than the promised minute, when he heard the click of a latch-key, and then a scuffling and stumbling sound from the passage, followed by an oath or two.

'Phœbe, Phœbe! I say!' the voice called out, 'is this a plant to break a fellow's shins?'

The owner of the voice looked in at the parlour-door for a moment, but, seeing nobody, went off again and ran upstairs.

'So that was Phœbe, I suppose,' thought Doyle. 'One of the Nelson family, I suppose. A pleasant household this seems to be at first sight—the gas cut off, and people who show they've come home by swearing at Phœbe. I've half a mind to be off again. If this is the way that Urquhart has taken to try experiments, and Ronaine to turn out a she-Phœnix, and Esdaile to do I forget what, and Bassett to do everything, I don't see why I should be bothered to turn out a decent shop-

N

girl or housemaid. I didn't pay my share that the admiral might get into trouble with the gas companies. But——'

His mind did not follow out the ' But,' which certainly could not have come to much, any way. But he had not made up his mind to escape by the time that the knocker sounded again. And, as neither the person who had sworn at Phœbe, nor anybody else, came to open it, Doyle was himself at last obliged to let Phœbe in again.

She did not apologise, but took a couple of candles from a newspaper, stuck them into a couple of bottles, after a good deal of balancing, and lighted them.

' It seems a bad fog,' said he.

' Yes; I nearly lost my way coming home. Please sit down,' she said, suddenly seeing the boots and throwing them into a corner. ' Father will be back any minute now.'

He sat down, while she began to lay out the tea, and was glad that this Phœbe did not resemble his idea of the child whom he did not know he saw in her.

It is true that this form of candlelight was not good for the study of a girl, beyond that one might look at her longer and more

steadily than daylight, or even London gas-
light, allows. But he saw that she was a
more than commonly pretty girl; and in his
view, beauty in a woman was the greatest
curse that nature could give her.

We have hitherto seen Phœbe with no
eyes at all, for her father's and her brothers',
even Phil's, were all too accustomed to her to
count for anything, and those of Stanislas
Adrianski, it may be presumed, were able to
see beauty wherever they might find sufficient
occasion. For poets are wizards, and can see
much where common eyes perceive nothing
but an income paid quarterly.

But Doyle, as a disinterested, or rather
absolutely uninterested, stranger saw her
simply as she was, and nothing less or more;
neither as one who, like Phil, knew her
faults and loved them; nor as one who, like
Stanislas, could know nothing of her but that
she was a good deal of a goose, whose eggs
might turn out to be at least of silver if not
of gold.

She was, as seen in the foggy candlelight
by Doyle, a bright-looking, rather fair-com-
plexioned girl; not short, though by no means
tall, slender, and graceful in every way. The

north London air had not given her depth or
height of colour, but it had not robbed her
of a delicate freshness which spoke well for
her health, and, despite all likelihood, of her
breeding.   Her hair, not too neatly arranged,
was of the very light tender shade of brown
which has no kindred with either flax or
gold ; it hung down in a delicate curly cloud
over her forehead, and brought out by contrast the darkness of nearly straight full eye-
brows, which of themselves were enough to
give her face a peculiar dramatic picturesque-
ness of its own.   The nose was rather small,
and slightly curved in the anti-aquiline
direction.   But anyhow it harmonised in
Phœbe's case with a fresh, sweetly-curved
mouth that was apt, by its silent speaking, to
show just the edges of the teeth, whether
smiling or grave.

Doyle, woman-scorner as he was, and non-
observant on principle, knew how to look at
pictures, and, just as on a picture, he looked at
Phœbe and saw what was to be seen.   The
mouth, he thought, was rather large and
generous for academic drawing, but it was
womanly in the best and sweetest way ; so
much so that, had he known the history or

rather mythology of her life he would have
wondered a good deal at the contrast between
the lips and the mind.

I, who hold all the doctrines of phy-
siognomy in sweeping contempt, do not
wonder at all; but physiognomists will know
what I mean.

He noticed, too, her fine little ears, like
ears, and not in the remotest degree like shells,
and the graceful turn of her slender neck,
which was not the least like a swan's—though
something of a goose's it may have been.

Lastly, strange to say, he tried to see
what her eyes were like; and, failing in his
first attempt, tried, as a matter of course, a
second time.

There was something mysteriously beautiful about Phœbe's eyes. They were rather
large, but the strong dark brows concealed
them a little, and their long dark lashes
veiled them a good deal more. They were
soft rather than bright—that could easily be
seen. But though Stanislas Adrianski, who
had looked into them both closely and deeply,
might know their colour, that secret defied
common and distant looking. They were not
black, they were not brown, they were cer-

tainly not blue. And so it seems to follow
that they must be grey—and perhaps they
were. But they were by no means of that
clear, constant, open grey that everybody
knows. They could soften into one shade, and
brighten into another, and then soften into a
third, and seemed to take as many expressions
in a second as there are seconds in an hour.
And change of expression means change of
light and change of shade, as all the world
knows ; and sometimes the change of shade
comes from quick change of thought and
feeling, while—' Sometimes,' thought Doyle,
' it's the other way round, and we fancy all
sorts of things behind the scenes because eyes
have a trick of changing : your fine windows
mean an empty house nine times out of ten.
But, all the same, that girl's face would be
her fortune—on the stage. . . . You are Mr.
Nelson's daughter ? ' asked he.

'Yes,' said Phœbe, thinking over her
garden-scene with Stanislas Adrianski.

'He has a large family, hasn't he ? '

'Who ? ' she asked, almost with a start :
for the question, coming upon the heel of her
thoughts, sounded like charging Stanislas
Adrianski with being the husband of that poor

creature, Natalie. 'Oh, you mean father. Yes, I suppose it is large. We have six boys, five at home,' she added with a sigh.

He could not help thinking her voice also a part of her beauty, for he was now, having once fallen into that track, observing her from a theatrical point of view. Bohemia was bringing back its own thoughts to the archdeacon. The voice was rich and soft, and yet full of character, and with a vibration that spoke of healthy strength and the power of making even a whisper, if it pleased, clearly heard.

'And no girl, then? None but yourself, I mean?'

'No.'

'But, surely, I should have thought you would have called yourselves sisters, you and——' He saw her puzzled look. 'Do you mean to say that no girl lives here but you?'

'But me? No.'

'Nor ever did?'

'Never. . . . I wish father would come home,' thought she.

'It is strange. I hope your father is not likely to be long? . . . This is strange,' he thought. 'Bassett, Urquhart, and now this fellow of an admiral. What can have become of the child? And where has my money gone? . . . I am interested in a girl of about your age. She would be now——'

A new light came into Phœbe's face. For weeks she had been dreaming the dream that the mystery of her birth and life were on the eve of being revealed. It was Stanislas Adrianski who had put it into her head, or at least had made the dream active, for it had always, more or less, been there. Her own mystery had always been a fancied sorrow, a real spring of pride. Everything had of late taken to happening. The foster-daughter of the Grand Robespierre, the betrothed of a hero of romance, the adopted daughter of Destiny! What was left to happen next but the revelation of the life to which she had been born? There was nothing strange to her in the manner of its coming. Nothing strange could possibly seem strange to her—for that matter, nothing had ever, except poor Phil's offer, seemed strange.

She was about to speak, though without knowing what she was about to say, when yet again the summons of 'Phœbe!' was heard from the front passage—this time in a high key that

the archdeacon would have recognised as the
admiral's had he heard it on the other side of
the world.   Phœbe ran out at once, and, after
a hurried word or two, led the admiral in.

'At last!' thought Doyle.  'There, at last,
is one thing that has not changed!'

He rose, but, till this mystery of the child
should be cleared up, did not hold out his
hand.

The archdeacon recognised the admiral at
once, but it was clear that the admiral had not
the faintest remembrance of the archdeacon.
And that might well be, for a big beard and a
heavy build are too common to swear to, and
no man on earth had, in all essential things,
within and without, changed more in all those
years than Doyle.

The admiral stood in a hovering sort of
attitude, and looked inquiringly.

'You   are   Mr.   Horatio   Collingwood
Nelson?' asked Doyle.

'The same.  I am.'   His visitor's voice
had evidently touched no memory.

'Then,' thought Doyle, 'I shall soon know
where I am.   I shall be able to ask questions
without getting answers that I sha'n't know to
be lies. . . . I have been asking for you at

your office—Mark and Simple, Gray's Inn Square. They gave me your address, here. I am acting for a friend who is engaged in an inquiry that interests him profoundly. Can you give me five minutes of your time—alone?'

The admiral looked at the tea-table, and sighed. But then he looked at the candles in the bottles, and sighed more deeply still. He was thirsty for his tea, but five minutes' private conversation might prove something he could ill afford to lose.

'Leave us, Phœbe,' said he.

She left the room, and did not think of listening at the keyhole. That is a thing that heroines of romance never do. Nor did she brave the fog and go into the garden. She could only go into the only room in the house that was fairly safe from invasion from the returned or returning boys—the room where Phil had used to sit up at night working—and wait in the dark, doing nothing, and thinking of too many things at once, and in too equal measure, for a girl who has just promised to be the wife of the man who, therefore, ought to be her whole world and her one thought—at any rate for a little while.

'I am come, ad—Mr. Nelson, on behalf of a friend of mine (I needn't mention names) who has found reason to think that somebody in the office of Mark and Simple might know something about a child that was lost in Gray's Inn Gardens a good many years ago.'

'Ah! H'm! Perhaps—— But, before we come to that, may I ask your name? Not necessarily for publication, but as a guarantee——'

'My name? I'll give you a name if you like—say Smith—for you to call me by; but, I tell you honestly, it won't be the real one. Well? You do know something of the matter, I see. I'll tell you how much I know and my friend knows. A matter known to six men at least isn't much of a secret, as you may suppose. Sir Charles Bassett, of Lincolnshire; Mr. Urquhart, a barrister; Mr. Esdaile, a painter; Mr. Ronaine, a surgeon; and a Mr. Doyle, charged themselves with the child's maintenance, and left her with you and your wife to bring up and take care of according to your views. Is the child alive? I asked Miss Nelson just now, and she told me she had never heard of the child!'

'Eh? That is a curious thing, now—a very curious thing. You have been asking Phœbe? And you tell me that Phœbe had never heard of such a thing? Very well, sir. I am in a position—none better—to satisfy any lawful gentleman, or lady, who is interested in this concern. To tell you the naked truth, I've been expecting some such inquiries all along. But it is but fair I should see my way clear, for, though I hold a political position as high as any going, I don't hold it for lucre, and, in some respects, I'm what may be called a struggling man. You might hardly think it, but I have had the child entirely on my hands.'

'What, with all that money paid for the child's maintenance? That is part of the history, mind. Do you mean to say that a man like Sir Charles Bassett——'

'Yes, sir, I do mean to say that a man like Sir Charles Bassett. He was like the child's grandfather at first—always turning up with toys and sugarplums. He brought her a wonderful thing that went by clock-work before she could walk, and Phil, one of my boys, took it all to pieces, and never could put it together again. It was about

the time my poor late wife had a cousin
staying with her to help her when my
youngest boy was born—an uncommonly
pretty girl. But that didn't last. After the
third quarter, Mr. Bassett—I should say Sir
Charles—went abroad, and there was an end
of him. He forgot all about it, I suppose.'

'I see. But the others——'

'Mr. Urquhart. He went on paying,
like that piece of clockwork, for years. But
I expect one day his wife got hold of his
cheque-book, or something; any way, there
was a row or a rumpus of some sort; and one
day Mr. Urquhart sent for me to his chambers,
and told me that he'd done all he could, and
really couldn't do any more. He gave me a
half-sovereign—that was before he was known
at the Bar—and I expect he hadn't a penny
in his pocket but what the grey mare allowed.
And that was an end of him.'

'And——?'

'Mr. Esdaile? Oh, he tumbled off a
scaffold and got killed, or something of that
kind. And Mr. Ronaine—nobody knows
what became of Mr. Ronaine. And Mr.
Doyle——'

'Well?'

'Well, sir, between me and you and all the world——— In fact, Mr. Doyle cut and run off to the West Indies, and there was an end of him.   Yellow fever, I daresay.'

Doyle, for a moment, felt a desire to take from his breast-pocket a pocket-book, and from the pocket-book the admiral's last receipt for the five pounds received from John Doyle just three months ago, and to confront the admiral with the evidence of his own lie.  But he thought delay would teach him more, and only asked :

'Then why have you kept the girl?'

'Well, it is difficult to answer that question in the way that a man of common-sense would understand.  But sentiment, sir, is a very wonderful thing; else why would you, or any other lady or gentleman, be asking after a girl who has been lost from time whereof the memory of man, as we say, runneth not to the contrary?  I have thought of things—advertising, and private detectives, and—but they're costly things ; and sentiment is cheap, sir; it is just the cheapest article alive.'

'Let me see the girl.'   He spoke sternly.

The admiral, with Phœbe's turn for fancy,

was beginning to wonder whether his visitor
might not turn out to be a peer in disguise.
And why should he own that Phœbe's little
fortune had been spent in trying to keep
his own wolf from his own door, or commit
himself to anything that might open up com-
munications with the absent and forgotten
Jack Doyle, and thus deprive him of this
annuity, welcome, though small, for evermore?
Phœbe had cost him nothing, for Phil, without saying a word to a soul about it, had contrived to pay for her clothes, and she had
saved him the cost of a maid of all work ever
since Mrs. Nelson had died.                    •

He went to the door. 'Phœbe!' he cried.

Phœbe smoothed her hair as well as she
could by the light of a lucifer-match, and
came slowly downstairs.

'This,' said the admiral, 'is Marion Eve
Psyche Zenobia Dulcibella Jane Burden, called
Phœbe for short because—well, because—
because it is not her name.'

## CHAPTER VIII

### FROM BOHEMIAN TO BARONET

IT will have been gathered, far more clearly than had been guessed by the archdeacon, that a very great change had happened in the life of him who had once upon a time been that best of good fellows, Charley Bassett, of Gray's Inn, and was now Sir Charles Bassett, of Cautleigh Hall, in Lincolnshire, for, in truth, the two men were one and the same. I say the two men on purpose, because for a man who counts his income by a few hundreds to be identical with one who reckons it by many thousands a year is clearly a social impossibility. He had no more dreamed of succeeding to his cousin's estates and title than he had of working for a living. Sir Mordaunt Bassett, whom he scarcely knew by sight, and was a little Bohemianly proud of not knowing, was unmarried, it is true. But he was of that period of middle life when marriage is more likely than in youth, or even than in old age, and it was exceedingly unlikely that, were Charley so much as his heir presumptive, he would keep single for the purpose of letting his title go to an unknown and not too respectable cousin. And, if the title had to go, he was not bound to refrain from making a will in order that the estates and the title might not be parted, while Charley was not his heir presumptive at all.

But Sir Mordaunt, though of an age when marriage is as likely and death as unlikely as such things can ever be, did not marry and did die. Not only so, but, by one of those chains of chance which so constantly link unlikely people with unexpected inheritances —and of which family histories are fuller than fiction, who is a timid creature, dares to be—baronetcy, land, and everything else worth mentioning, came to Charley. Genealogies, except to heirs themselves, are notoriously disagreeable and uninteresting things, nor had his own been particularly interesting to Charley hitherto. It had been for his friends, not for himself, to remember that he was first cousin to Sir Mordaunt Bassett of

Cautleigh Hall. But now he found cause to be exceedingly interested in Sir Mordaunt's brother, the rector of Cautleigh, who caught cold at the funeral, and died after a baronetcy of three weeks, without leaving behind him so much as a widow. His solicitors—naturally his old landlords, Messrs. Mark and Simple, of Gray's Inn Square—still further interested him by the story of how yet a third brother, of whom he had known still less, had died at sea a very short time before, and how an uncle, whose issue had senior claims to the branch which Charley represented, had forgotten to put his children into their proper position by marrying their mother. The family history of the Bassetts, when it came to be turned over, appeared a little peculiar in many ways, and complex enough to require some expensive and rather troublesome looking into. But the end was simple enough. Neither will, nor settlement, nor claim, nor question stood between Charley Bassett and one of the best things in England.

The event caused a good deal of stir in the late Sir Mordaunt's part of Lincolnshire. But it was nothing to the excitement in Charley's corner of Bohemia. Would he

remain there still? Would he take a new
house, and keep it open for the benefit of his
old friends? Would five-pound notes be fly-
ing about as freely as half-crowns? Before
he was two days older he received as many
visits from men who were nobody's enemies
but their own as if he had just been made
Prime Minister. He was at home to them all,
and more genial than ever. But he answered
the general question in his own way. He
said nothing about what he was going to do
with his good luck, but pinned a piece of
paper on his door with this legend, 'Mr.
Bassett will be back in a quarter of an hour.'
And there it remained, to the huge enjoyment
of all the clerks of Messrs. Mark and Simple,
till the quarters had grown into hours and
the hours into days and the days into weeks.
That quarter of an hour never expired. Sir
Charles Bassett was travelling abroad; and
neither into Gray's Inn Square nor into
Bohemia did Charley Bassett ever return.
And in nine days the generation which had
known him forgot him, except when it needed
some unattainable half-crown. He left behind
him neither an enemy nor a friend.

A fellow like Doyle might wonder at the

easy way in which so easy-going a man should
forget so easy an obligation as that which he
had undertaken towards Marion Eve Psyche
Zenobia Dulcibella Jane Burden.   But people
of ordinary sense and knowledge will see how
unfair it would be towards Sir Charles Bassett
to expect him, in the midst of new and all-
absorbing business, to remember every little
jocular folly of which he might have been
guilty when he had only some three or four
hundred a year.   He forgot a great many
more important things.   He forgot to finish
a picture and a comedy.   He forgot, and was
not at much pains to avoid forgetting, Jack
Doyle, who was essentially the sort of man
for a country gentleman not to know, and,
naturally enough, did not think it needful to
solder with gold the trifling link that bound
them together.   Lawyers, land-stewards, and
all sorts of respectable people took up a good
deal of his time while he was abroad ; and,
when he came at last to his new home in
Lincolnshire, he never quite realised that he
was the man who had once luxuriously starved
for the whole year on what was now not a
single month's income.   After all, it was
because he liked being first, rather than for

anything else, that he had lived in a country
where a very few hundred a year would make
him first without trouble. He simply rose to
the occasion, and felt that his title and its
accompaniments would be wasted in keeping
the first place in Gray's Inn Square, when it
might make him a Triton among Tritons
instead of among minnows. As constantly
happens in Bohemia, and elsewhere, the men
who thought they knew Charley Bassett, that
prince of easy-going, good-natured fellows,
knew him no more than they knew themselves. And, when it took wind in his
solicitors' office that Sir Charles Bassett was
going to be married to his neighbour in the
country, Miss Florence Lanyon, Mr. Lanyon
of Hawlby's second daughter, the office wag
changed the notice on the door, so as to make
it read ' Gone to be haltered. Friends will
please to accept this intimation.' It was the
only intimation of his change of life that any
of his old friends ever received. He asked
to the wedding, as his best man, neither
Urquhart, nor Esdaile, nor Ronaine, nor
Doyle. He did not think it needful to explain
to his bride's family that he had a sixth share
in the fatherhood of a little girl. Harmless

as such jokes may be, they make people in
counties whisper unkind things.

He had sown his wild oats, and, as landlord, master, magistrate, husband, and father,
left nothing to be desired. If you want to
make a Philistine of the Philistines, give a
Bohemian a great many thousands a year.
He will become a ruler in Gath and a prince
in Ascalon. Indeed, by the time he was five-
and-thirty, Sir Charles began to show signs of
economy which, though not amounting to
more than laudable thrift, would have been
much more natural in the days when he used
to spend every penny of his income every
year. It is upon somebody else's horse, not
his own, that a mounted beggar rides to the
devil; and, for that matter, Sir Charles had
never been really a beggar, though he had
always taken a Bohemian pride in calling
himself one, and now really thought so. His
steward, his bankers, and his stockbrokers
knew that he was a richer man every year, in
the safest and most real ways. Nobody could
accuse him of being a whit fonder of music,
painting, or poetry, than his neighbours. If
he had only taken to any form of killing
birds or beasts, or of any other form of bodily

exercise, he would have been absolutely the most respectable baronet in that part of England. But, by the time he was forty, even his bodily indolence ceased to be remarkable. He was already getting stout, and a little grey and bald ; and his son and heir had arrived at an age supremely interesting to the mothers of many daughters.

Ralph Bassett was always said to be very like his father. And so he was, with a likeness that increased every year, but also with a difference that increased likewise. For one thing, he had always known from his cradle that he was heir to a splendid estate and a title, and had never, till he went to Oxford, known what it means to be one's own master. If ever there was a father who wished to save a son from his own youthful fancies and follies, Sir Charles Bassett was that man. Ralph was a good fellow enough, with lively spirits, amiable manners, a superb temper, and quite enough abilities to serve a rich and unambitious man ; he would have been regarded as a swan by nine fathers out of ten. And yet he managed to keep on disappointing his father at every turn. He was liked about the place, and at school, and at Oxford, and, in spite of his popularity, never fell into any scrape worth mentioning ; but it seemed to Sir Charles that he would never grow into a man—that he would always remain a boy. From his father's increasingly severe point of view, Oxford had been a failure, and so, to keep him from idling about Cautleigh with guns or girls, or travelling all over England with bat and ball, or playing at soldiers, he decided upon making a barrister of him, as a preparation for the heavy legal responsibilities he would sooner or later have to incur as a justice of the peace for Lincolnshire—perhaps as a legislator for the British Empire.

Now, it so happened that, making inquiries of Mr. Simple with that view, he was told of Mr. Urquhart as a gentleman eminently qualified to teach the whole art and mystery of legal practice during such stray minutes of leisure as he could find in about six months of the year. Of course Sir Charles Bassett recognised the name, and he remembered all the peculiarities of the experimental philosopher. A long, dormant sentiment warmed his heart to a friend of his youth who had succeeded in life, and with whom friendship might, without the least inconvenience, be renewed.

When Sir Charles Bassett, of Cautleigh
Hall, and Robert Urquhart, of the Home
Circuit, grasped hands, they were really glad
to meet again. When they dined together at
Sir Charles's club they talked over a hundred
old recollections, and even wondered what
had become of that poor devil, Jack Doyle.
He had drunk himself to death, they supposed, and voted him an epitaph the reverse
of complimentary. But about Marion Eve
Psyche Zenobia Dulcibella Jane Burden neither
spoke a word. After all, she had been but
the slightest of episodes. As Urquhart, for
domestic reasons, did not touch upon a topic
that had been an unpleasant one, Sir Charles
took for granted that his friend had practically forgotten the sixfold bond as completely
as he ; and, in any case, what good or pleasure
could come of asking, ' I wonder what has
become of that godchild of ours? Has our
forgetfulness brought her to the workhouse,
or the streets, or where? Or am I the only
one who has forgotten, except you, who
would surely mention the matter if you had
not kept me in countenance by forgetting
too? Or have we been throwing the whole
burden on old friends who, ten to one, have

not become rich baronets or eminent barristers?' Such a question would be too suggestive for any man who respected himself to
put to anybody in a like position; so mutual
courtesy and consideration forbade its being
made. The baronet knew too much; the
barrister preferred not to know anything
at all.

Urquhart cordially accepted the usual fee
for giving his old friend's son the run of his
chambers and of his papers, and asked Sir
Charles to dine with him at home, to be introduced to Mrs. Urquhart, who received her
guest with all the cordiality due to her husband's oldest and dearest friend. She had
often heard him speak of Sir Charles Bassett,
of Cautleigh Hall, and, to tell the truth, had
incredulously wondered in her heart at the
story of an intimacy between so great a per-
sonage and anybody in the position in which
she knew her husband to have been as a
young man. It was a sort of husband's victory to prove his position by actually bringing
his lion home. Nor afterwards, when her
hospitality was extended to Ralph on his
arrival in town, had he any reason to complain of the coldness which had, even in his

anger, so much impressed Doyle. Nor did he complain; but, nevertheless, when he was next asked to dinner in Fonthill Gardens he arranged for a previous engagement, which obliged him to refuse. At any rate he was like his father in one thing—he always managed, and always with grace, to avoid doing anything that was not exactly the very pleasantest to him at the time. He liked ladies, and it struck him that Mrs. Urquhart was not a lady. He also liked a great many women who did not pretend to be ladies; but then Mrs. Urquhart did pretend. Nor could he manage to make out how his father and Urquhart, the husband, could ever at any time have been real friends. But that often strikes outsiders as queer in the case of middle-aged gentlemen who, once upon a time, were young. The time might yet come when the story of an ancient friendship between Ralph and Lawrence, commonplace as it was, might make their descendants stare. Why are moralists so hard on those who drift apart from their old friends, and are always making new? Would they make friendship hinder growth, which must needs mean change? Orestes and Pylades, David and

Jonathan, did not outgrow youth together. Urquhart and Bassett had passed their forty years.

So Ralph Bassett, without the least intention of becoming Lord Chancellor, or even of prosecuting a thief at his county sessions, lived very much in the manner he had told his friend Lawrence, troubling Urquhart exceedingly little and himself not at all. Like his father before him, he had a great many acquaintances, and the circle kept on growing. He found a great many of his Oxford set in town, and he did not find those of them who had their homes in London shy of introducing him to their people, including their sisters. Like most of the Oxford men of his time, he had the fancy for making himself out to be a great deal worse in every way than he was in reality, to make a show of faults that belonged in reality to other people, and to hide his better qualities as if they were sins; a form of hypocrisy which is for some reason or other considered graceful. It led him into some small and unimportant follies for the sake of keeping up his reputation. But on the whole it seemed likely that he would drift along very safely as well as very pleasantly until

nature should make him a baronet, and that
he would then drift along in the same manner
until nature should pass on the title to his
own son, without doing any particular harm
to himself and none to the world.

He did not act upon Lawrence's sugges-
tion, and think seriously about that story of
the girl with six fathers which he had heard
in the railway train. And yet it had struck
him more than a little disagreeably. It had
seemed odd that his father, seeing what he
was now, should ever have been mixed up
with underbred people like the Urquharts;
but that there should ever have been any
connection between Sir Charles Bassett and a
man of the archdeacon's reputation seemed
contrary to the nature of things. The untold
story, whatever it might turn out to be, appeared to have about it a flavour of something wrong; and then Urquhart's name also
had been dragged into it, a matter that seemed
even more strange. Of course Lawrence's
suspicions were absurd. What hold could
any creature have upon Sir Charles Bassett,
of Cautleigh Hall? But still, on thinking of
the matter when it came into his head next
morning, during the half hour between

waking and rising, he considered whether it
might not be as well to write a letter to his
father about things in general in order to
introduce his slight adventure with the archdeacon. But the second thoughts which
came after breakfast led him to a different
conclusion. Such a letter, being troublesome
to write to-day, would keep perfectly well till
to-morrow, and the idea of pumping his father,
or of seeming to imagine that he could possibly need a warning, was more unpleasant
than even writing a letter. So he did what
he was very nearly as little in the habit of
doing as he had told Lawrence. He actually
went to chambers about lunch-time, and
amused himself with a novel until about five
o'clock, when Urquhart came back from
Westminster, or wherever his day's work may
have lain.

'What—Bassett!' said Urquhart, shaking
his head with an air of humorous rebuke.
'Now, it's a strange thing, but I was thinking
of you only the other day—I suppose by a
sort of association of ideas. I'm off to-morrow,
for the arbitration in Green and Gray, ye
know—or I'm sadly afraid ye don't know. I
don't expect I'll be back for some time. But

I'll leave ye a case to look up, that came in only to-day——'

'Thank you,' said Ralph, closing his novel. 'I happened to be passing, so I thought I'd look in to see how things are going on. I've just come back from Switzerland.'

'From Switzerland!' Urquhart, of all Phœbe's fathers, had, next to the admiral, changed the least of all. Whatever he might be at home, in the hands of Mrs. Urquhart, he retained in the citadel of his own chambers, as well as in Court, all that aquiline look and dogmatic manner which, with a little formal logic and a shilling or two, had represented the whole of his stock when he first opened accounts with the world. 'From Switzerland! Then ye've not even seen the papers in Gray and Green. It's a pity. Ye can see Switzerland any day; but Gray and Green——'

'I don't know,' said Ralph. 'It seems to me as if Gray and Green came into existence before the Jungfrau, and will outlast the Matterhorn. Mrs. Urquhart is well, I hope. By the way, I happened to meet, coming up, a man who used to know you——'

'Ah! Who was he?'

'A man named Doyle. And a queer sort of customer he seemed.'

'Doyle? Doyle?' asked Urquhart, passing his fingers through his hair, as if trying to remember the name. 'I never knew but one Doyle; and your father, Sir Charles, knew him too. But it isn't likely to be he.'

'He did say he knew my father too,' said Ralph, 'when they were young men. He said he had been in India——'

Ralph could see that Urquhart began to look annoyed.

'That fellow turned up again!' he exclaimed. 'I hope, Bassett, ye didn't tell him where I live? He just was a poor fellow Sir Charles and I used to know, and who, we thought, had drunk himself out of the world long and long ago. Did he ask ye, as your father's son, to lend him half-a-crown, for the sake of auld lang syne?'

'On the contrary, he looked to me like a man much more likely to lend half-crowns; and from what Lawrence—a man who was with me, and knew him in India—told me, lending seems to be very much in his line. Then you think my father won't say "thank you" if I re-introduce him to an old friend?'

'Well, since you ask me, I don't think he will. Anyhow, Bassett, I'll be obliged if ye won't re-introduce him to me. He's not the man, ye understand, that I'd like Mrs. Urquhart to know.'

'What did he mean by the story of a child with six fathers?'

'Eh? A child with six fathers? Ye'll excuse me, Bassett, but I must get home early to-day, and I'm off for the North to-morrow. Whatever that fellow told ye is safe to be a pack of lies. There's no liar like a man that drinks—none.'

Urquhart, from the depths of his domestic terrors, spoke so feelingly that Ralph left the chambers convinced that there was something wrong.

## CHAPTER IX

### AT THE PLAY

'But I do think you ought just to mention the matter to Sir Charles, all the same,' said Lawrence, over an after-breakfast cigar in Ralph's rooms. 'I've knocked about the world a good bit, and I've got my suspicions. Suspicions are as often wrong as right, of course; but they're—well, I've found mine quite as often right as wrong. There's been something up, somewhere or other, between your governor, and Urquhart, and my archdeacon. And so——'

'You mean to suspect,' exclaimed Ralph, 'that my father—— By Jupiter Ammon, Lawrence, if anybody else had put things in that way—had talked of suspecting my father of anything you can name—I think he'd have had to know how hot coffee feels outside! What the deuce do you mean?'

'Come, old fellow, don't be volcanic—

it's bad form. Of course I wouldn't talk of
suspecting Sir Charles Bassett, or any people
of yours, of anything a gentleman wouldn't
do, or that would put him in the dock, or
that sort of thing. But there isn't a man
going that some rascal mayn't think he's got
some sort of a hold over. Mind, I don't say
has got a hold, but thinks he's got a hold ;
and the way to treat him is to tell him to go
to the deuce at once, and tell his story there.
But you can't tell him to go anywhere unless
you know he's somewhere, and has got a story
to tell. I know the world, and I've been in
scrapes myself, and I hope to be in a good
many more. If I came across a black sheep
who said he'd got an old story about you,
I should let you know. I don't see why
you should treat a fellow badly because he
happens to be your governor. Just let him
know you've tumbled over a party of the
name of Doyle, and then, depend upon it,
he'll know what to do.'

'Well, I suppose you're right. Not to
do it would look like—something or other—
like seeming as if one was afraid of one's
father's being afraid of somebody or something. But how about the child with all the

fathers. Ought I to mention that, or let it alone?'

'Not knowing how far you and he are on chaffing terms, I don't know. My father does not understand chaff, but yours may.'

'I'll write, then, to-morrow—no, to-day, while I'm in the mood. I'll do it now. I'll ask for a cheque, or else he'll think it queer.'

'Lucky fellow that you are! By the way, do you mind being bothered with a girl?'

'I? That depends on the nature of the bother and the niceness of the girl. Come, don't interrupt an author in the thick of inspiration. I meant to ask for fifty pounds, and you've made me write five hundred.'

'Moral—you see what nothings may turn out to be. Never mind; if you don't know what to do with the difference, I'm your man. I'm bothered with a girl. I've got a sister Fanny up in town, and I've got to take her to the play. That's what they call it in the country—"to the play." Come too. Doing disagreeable things is good for the soul, but it isn't good for the soul to do them all alone. Besides, I don't know where to take a respectable young woman, and you do.'

'Of course I do. "Your affectionate son,

Ralph." I don't object to respectable young women at all. I know several sisters who are really quite nice, and no trouble at all. I rather like being chaperon. Let me see. I can't to-morrow, nor Tuesday, nor Wednesday. Thursday—yes, 'Olga' on Thursday. Feed here with me, and we'll fetch Miss Fanny and go.'

' "Olga!" Is that the piece where your bayadère does the double-shuffle or the *pas de* whatever her Natch is called in London? Ah! the sacrifice won't be so vast after all.'

Ralph, for all his professions of advanced manliness, coloured.

'Double-shuffles be hanged! Nelly's one thing, and Miss Lawrence is another,' he said, as awkwardly as if he were the rawest of schoolboys. 'One doesn't mix things. I know some men do, but it's awfully bad form. No; Nelly's not in "Olga." You needn't be afraid.'

Lawrence had not been in the least afraid, and he first stared, then smiled a little, from some superior height, at such old-fashioned scruples in a man who was no older in mere years than he. But he said nothing. He liked the future Sir Ralph Bassett so much that he would sooner have him for a brother-in-law than any man he knew.

The letter was written; and in due course, that is to say on Thursday, Ralph received this answer from Sir Charles:

'MY DEAR BOY,—You have certainly learned one thing in Urquhart's chambers: the art of coming to the point, and making other people come to it also. You will find enclosed my cheque for the sum you say you want—namely, fifty pounds; and, as you don't tell me what you want it for, I won't ask you. I was sorry you put off coming back from Switzerland so long that you had to go straight to London instead of going there *viâ* home, and I can't quite agree with you (I wish I could) that Urquhart could not, without your immediate personal assistance, have dealt with the difficulties of Gray and Green.

' Please to remember that it is a century at least since the heavy father in the country made a point of believing everything that he heard from his son in town. You don't tell me much (to say the least of it) of your Swiss tour; but I can quite believe there was nothing to tell. It takes a clever fellow to

say anything new about the genus Cockney,
which is, I believe, the principal production
now to be found in that country of patriotic
publicans, who find their native land so dear,
that they can't rest till they have made
foreigners find it still dearer. But you have
a sign of grace—you don't retail guide-book
gush, and you don't think it interesting to
set down how high you have carried an unbroken neck above the level of the sea. Only
if you didn't carry these common objects
with you, why go at all? For I don't suppose you carried any particular object of
your own, unless to give Blackstone a holiday, which, I'm afraid, was the carrying of
coals to Newcastle. I wish I could think
you were using your time. I was no idler
in London, I can tell you, in my time. By
the way, you say you have come across a
man by the name of Doyle, who claims acquaintance with me. I did have some knowledge of a literary ragamuffin named Doyle,
who I thought had gone to the dogs, and
died there, long ago. And, *à propos* of Doyle
and cheques (if this Doyle be that Doyle) if
he tries to scrape up an acquaintance with
you, on the strength of having now and then

drunk at my expense, don't let him. He's
not a man to know. He's the kind of man
who does not vanish when you've lent him
half-a-crown. It's the half-crown that vanishes
—not he. So he told you that story about
the child in Gray's Inn. It was really rather
a curious one. I'll tell it you some day. I'd
forgotten it myself till your letter brought it
back to me. Just as a matter of curiosity,
ask Simple if he ever gives work now to a
sort of an odd job clerk of the name of Nelson ;
and ask Nelson if he happens to know what
has become of a girl named Marion Burden.
From what I remember of Doyle, I don't like
the notion of his turning up at this time of
day, and taking so warm an interest in men
whom he thinks may be worth looking after.
A man like that always ends in one of two
ways—he either drinks himself to death, or
else he drinks himself into an unscrupulous
scoundrel. Nelson was a sort of an idiot,
not likely to improve by keeping ; so you see
it might possibly be prudent to hear what
the idiot has to say before the blackguard
gets hold of him ; a girl, for whose bringing
up I once paid (till I was firm enough to
refuse to be bled any more), might be a card

in the hands of an idiot and a knave. Of
course they could do nothing really, and I
need not tell you that the story you will hear
from me and (if he tells the truth) from Nelson
might be published from the housetops for
anything I care. But, as it might be twisted,
I should like to know what Nelson has to say
of his own motion.—God bless you.

'Your affectionate

' FATHER.'


It could not possibly strike Ralph, knowing
nothing of the circumstances, that it was in
the least strange for Sir Charles Bassett, after
carelessly ignoring every sort of connection
with his old life for a whole generation, to
suddenly show an interest in what, not being
serious, must needs be the merest of trifles.
Nor did he suppose it to be more than a trifle.
But he was naturally struck by the coincidence
between Lawrence's piece of guess-work and
character-reading and his father's views of
things. This Doyle was evidently a dangerous
man, to be kept at arm's length. Nobody—
and the best of men least—can afford to laugh
at a lie. So that very morning he asked after
Mr. Nelson at Mark & Simple's. As it hap-

pened, however, Mr. Nelson was out on some errand, and would not be back for at least an hour; and it also happened that, on that particular Thursday, hours were to Ralph precious things. He had to dine earlier than usual, to go with Lawrence and his sister to the theatre, and he had to dress before dinner, and he had to take a ride before dressing, and before that he had to see a man about a dog for a lady, and to order some cigars, and several equally important matters to attend to; and neither the next day nor the next would he be able to be near Gray's Inn at all. So, struck by a happy thought, he left this note to be given to the clerk on his return from his errand.

'Sir Charles Bassett wishes to make inquiries after Marion Burden. Will Mr. Nelson kindly call to-morrow (Friday) evening at the above address, and give what information he can? Any time between five and seven.'

Being in a hurry, and being nothing of a detective, the message was neither so judiciously nor so clearly worded as it might have been, and rather mixed up its actual writer with the writer's father. But of course it did well enough, saved a great deal of bother, and enabled Ralph to send word to his father sooner than, owing to urgent private engagements, would have been otherwise possible. He was equally successful, or at least equally satisfied with himself, in the matter of the dog, and of the cigars. Then he rode, dressed, met Lawrence at the club, dined, and then went to take up Miss Lawrence at the relations' with whom she was staying, but who, as they never went out anywhere, were of no manner of use to a country cousin.

Fanny Lawrence proved to be a lively and commonly pretty girl, of that too quickly fleeting age when a girl, not to be pretty enough, must be very plain indeed, and Ralph took a fancy to her at first sight, as was his usual way with women whose beauty was not so great as to give them the right to make themselves disagreeable. For that matter, that was the last right she was in a mood to claim, for she was simple enough to look upon a play as a treat, and upon her brother as a truly great as well as admirable young man ; and yet not so simple as to look down upon a brother's friend, who would be some day Sir Ralph, and was, meanwhile, as handsome and nice as if he were only a younger son and captain in the Guards.

Whether she was interested in ' Olga ' or

not I cannot tell, for she was by no means one of those uncomfortable *ingénues* of fiction who so sadly bore their companions by having no eyes or ears for anybody or anything but the stage. From first taking her seat, and after as well as before the curtain rose, she had eyes for everybody and everywhere, down to the very sticks that had rattled on the big drum ; and she could hear and smile at Ralph's very smallest joke in the middle of the most thrilling scene. She did not even refrain from making original remarks on her own account, without any of that painful shyness which makes some people suspect that their companions may possibly prefer the words of the play, at least for the time, to theirs, however witty or profound. She did not wait till the end to criticise, and her criticism took a free and wide range.

'Look at that man playing the very big fiddle !' whispered she, while slow music was accompanying some climax of action. 'Why doesn't he cut his hair ? And why does he wear that long piece of black plaster nearly down to his nose ? '

'The eccentricities of genius, I suppose,' said Ralph.

' I wonder what it feels like,' said Fanny.
' Don't you ? '

' What feels like ?  You don't mean about
having long hair, because I suppose you know
that very well.  Like having a plaster down
your nose ? '

' How absurd you are !  Like being a genius,
I mean.  A genius for playing on a really large
fiddle, or for painting, or poetry, or things
that people have genius for.  But look at those
people up in that box.  Do you call her pretty ?
I dare say she is, but——'

' Up there ? ' asked Ralph, obediently looking vaguely upwards.  ' Well—no—if it comes
to that, I can't say I do.  She strikes me as
being a little too fat and red, and a great deal
too old for perfect beauty.  Still, there may
be some men who admire that style——'

' Fat—red—old ?  You must be looking
wrong.  Oh, I see who you mean !  Look,
Frank—look at what Mr. Bassett says some
people call pretty ! '  The curtain had fallen
now upon the last act but one, so that conversation might flow more freely.  ' I mean up
there—that rather fair girl in white with that
man with a large beard.'

' And, by Jove ! ' said her brother, ' if

Bassett says some people call that girl pretty,
I'm one of them.   She's the only girl I've seen
worth looking at since I've been home.   Why,
she must have come straight from India——'

'Oh, Frank! What—with that complexion
and that light sort of hair?   Why, you must
be looking wrong too.'

'Nonsense, Fanny.   I don't mean the
niggers.   I mean the English girls.   They're
always prettier out in India than they are before they go out, or when they come home——'

'Yes; if only six blackberries came in a
season, how people would rave about them,
to be sure!   Last year, when we had more
peaches than we could eat, we turned up our
noses at them.   That girl must have been
eating too many peaches, I'm afraid.   Mr.
Bassett, which way do you like a nose to turn?'

Ralph glanced at Fanny's nose, and said,
'If anything, just a trifle down,' and was rewarded with a bright smile.

'I don't pick beauty to bits,' said Lawrence.
'She is just lovely—nose and all.   Greeks and
Romans always bring back the bad side of my
school days, and Jews—but talking of Jews—
by Jove!   Bassett, look at the man with her!
Don't you see?'

Fanny, of course, looked up the quickest, and saw the big man with the big beard lean forward, so that his face could be seen clearly. But she was much more interested in examining the points of a girl who came up so completely to her brother's fastidious taste in beauty. And just then the girl also leaned forward; and, as she did so, Fanny, through her opera-glass, saw her start, and then half draw back, and then colour hotly all over. Was it a recognition? Had her brother any special reason for declaring her to be absolutely lovely, even to the point of her nose? But, following in her lightning-like way the invisible chain that is forged of starts and glances, she saw, not her brother, but the plastered fiddler staring up at the box with all his eyes, and that the straightest of invisible lines ran from his to the girl's, and back again. A man would have seen nothing of all this. But Fanny knew by instinct that she was being favoured with an extra scene by way of interlude to 'Olga.' And she had made it all out before Ralph had time to exclaim:

'The archdeacon, by Jove!'

'I told you he was a dark sort of customer. Fancy him going about with a creature like that—that won't do. Money's money, worse luck; but I'm not going to stand that sort of thing. As sure as my name's Frank Lawrence, I won't go home to-night without knowing that girl's name.'

Fanny was beginning to feel curious, and Ralph to think that this kind of talk before one's sister was hardly up to his friend's usual good form. But the last act compelled the fiddler back to his bow, and obliged the three to be decently silent—so that for the present nothing more could come of the adventure, if such Lawrence intended it to be. The girl sat rather more back in her box, looked steadfastly on the stage, and used her fan a great deal. But as soon as the play was over, Lawrence managed to hurry his party out, and, without seeming to have any purpose, to bring them to a stand in the passage until the boxes were cleared. They had not been there more than a minute when the man with the beard, the girl on his arm, passed by.

'Ah!' he said, affecting a slight start of genial surprise. 'We fellow Indians seem destined to tumble over one another in trains, and theatres, and everywhere. Do you remember giving me a very seasonable lecture

the other day? And you remember your
friend Sir Charles Bassett's son? If Mrs. Doyle
is new to England,' he said, covering the
impudence of his self-introduction with the
politest and most deferential of bows, ' she
must have found the inside of a London theatre
worth seeing.' Not that his impudence was
very great in his own opinion, for he looked
upon the archdeacon as the fairest of all possible game, and upon the girl as both easier
as well as fairer. ' Can I see after your
carriage? Or——'

' My daughter, Miss Phœbe Doyle,' said
the archdeacon, correcting the error in the
shortest and quietest way he could, and passed
on without another word.

' His daughter!' said Lawrence thoughtfully. ' Miss Phœbe Doyle. I'll remember
that name. The archdeacon may be an uncomfortable creditor to one's friends, poor
devils! but for that very reason he ought to
make a first-rate father-in-law.'

' Yes, Lawrence,' said Ralph, ' you're
about right. She is a lovely girl.' For which
speech Miss Fanny did not reward him with a
smile.

' And her nose does turn up,' said she.

When Ralph returned home he found a letter upon his table, which ran as follows:

'49 Gray's Inn Square.

'SIR,—I have the honour to regret that it will be useless for me to honour myself by paying my respects to you. In answer to your inquiries, I have to inform Sir Charles Bassett of the late lamented death—many years ago—through a fatal illness, of Miss Marion Eve Psyche Zenobia Dulcibella Jane Burden. I have the honour to remain, Sir Charles, yours obediently (without prejudice to principle),

'HORATIO COLLINGWOOD NELSON,

'G.P.A.R.'

# CHAPTER X

### THE BEGINNING OF PHŒBE DOYLE

THINK how things had gone with Phœbe from the beginning ; and ask if they must not have been like a dream—like a page torn out from the second, that is to say the most bewilderingly complicated, volume of one of her familiar story-books, and applied to herself in a way that out-dreams dreams.

She had risen in the morning without the prospect of anything more exciting than a silent conversation with that withered bush which stood for the symbol of a dead and empty life, that had to depend upon fancy for all its leaves and blossoms, until fancy itself, from over-work, should become even more barren and sapless than reality.

She had to conjure a ruler of nations out of a pot-house orator, a hero of romance and liberty out of a threadbare fiddler, and a mysterious heroine out of herself; and though it was all easy enough at present, she could not, in her heart of hearts, expect the soil on which she and her bush stagnated together to give them food for new sap every day—rainy days and all. Quite enough little things had lately happened to make the freshly tasted excitement of something in the shape of real food a sort of second necessity. It was as yet no less easy than it had always been to feast on fancies, but she had tasted the salt of real looks and of real words, and this had made the flavour of unsalted fancies feel pointless and poor.

It was thus she had begun her day. By nightfall she knew that she had given her whole self to Stanislas Adrianski ; before night the mystery of her life had been unveiled. Stanislas Adrianski had, in his knightly and masterful fashion, wooed and won, not Phœbe Burden, a struggling law-clerk's foster-foundling, but Phœbe Doyle, the acknowledged daughter and heiress of a rich stranger who had at last come back from beyond the seas to do justice and to find and claim his own.

And yet, dreamlike as it ought to have been, it was all more right and natural to Phœbe than a commonplace flirtation in a

ball-room would have been to ninety-nine
girls in a hundred.   Phœbe was the hundredth
girl.   If the veil had been torn from the
mystery of her birth to show her, standing
within the shrine of home-love, some mere
grocer or market-gardener, or any other
honest but uninteresting person, she would
have thought it strange, and have preferred the
enjoyment of an unbroken and undiminished
mystery.   It was, at any rate, something not
utterly vapid and ignominious to be the
adopted daughter and confidante of a chief of
Associated Robespierres, whose taste for tea
and shrimps was merely a great man's foible,
and would therefore, as such, fill a respectable
corner of the world's history in time to come.
She had already read 'Shrimps, His Liking
for, page four hundred and seventy-three,' in
the uncompiled index to an unwritten bio-
graphy of Horatio Collingwood Nelson.   But
the story that parted her old life from her
new did not seem to her strange at all.

'We call her Phœbe—because it is not her
name.'

These were the first words of which her
ears were conscious when she came downstairs from her bedroom, and felt, with her

only too quick and ready instinct—as quick and ready as a flight of fancy—that the distinguished-looking stranger of middle age and with the big beard, whose acquaintance she had already made, held the key to the secret of her birth and destiny. So they had been talking about her. Who was she? What was she to be?

'So!' said he. 'So this is the child who has been thrown upon charity by her own people, and whom charity has forgotten. I don't blame you, Mr. Nelson,' he said with a certain contemptuous indifference in his tone, not thinking it worth while to express his opinion of a man whom he had mentally convicted of a mean lie to cover a petty fraud. 'You have done more than your duty——'

'Pray don't mention it,' said the admiral. 'It is what England expects of every man.'

'And so you have doubtless expected more than your pay. It is not right you should lose——'

'Ah! If every man,' said the admiral modestly, 'if every man had his deserts, as I always say——'

'And so you shall not lose.'

Here, he felt and knew now, was he, after a long, lonely, weary term of exile, undertaken and (till habit and success had hardened and warped it into other grooves) maintained for this very girl's sake, returned to find himself alone true to a compact which he had been taking for the one link that bound him to his fellow men. Lawrence would have allowed him no right to feelings too fine to be measured by gold.

But it may well be that even a usurer has depths beyond the reach of the philosophy of the very cleverest of young men. He knew— none else can guess—what that compact had come to mean to him. He himself had never known what it had meant till now, when he found how little it had meant to other men, whom it had never cost a moment's struggle against self or a single act of self-denial.

It was for a chance promise made to a chance baby-girl that he had performed the miracle of changing his nature, whether for good or for ill. Whatever the means, it was for that baby-girl's sake that he had ceased to be whatever he had been, and had become whatever he had become; as much and as truly for her sake as other men crush them-

selves, with loving good-will, under the lighter
labours that have wives and children for their
comfort, and the welfare of wives and children
for their ample reward. If it had not been
for the one duty of sending a few pounds a
year to England what would his life in India
have been? It had been lived alone; but,
save for this seeming nothing, it would have
been lived absolutely, unsurpassably alone.
And now it all turned out to have been a
stupid blunder. Nobody else concerned had
cared a straw about the matter, and he had
bothered with throwing away so much
capital—so his reason, ashamed as usual of
his heart, chose to put it—to help a silly
knave to pay his rent and to stave off the
reprisals of a gas company; perhaps, and
probably, to save the expense of a cook and
housemaid. The lost capital had not been
much, it is true, but the principle was the
same.

'And we, calling ourselves, some of us,
gentlemen, have united together only to
make a present of this child's life to that
fellow, who is evidently only just saved from
being a whole rogue by being more than half
a fool,' he thought to himself, while bending

his eyes upon Phœbe in such wise as, without meaning her to be aware of their gaze, to make her feel less excited than confused and shy. Who could he be? Ought that voice of nature, of which stories tell us so much, to command her to exclaim something or other and to fall into his open arms? It is true his arms were not open; but then, if they had been, the voice of nature was as stupidly dumb as usual. 'Of course, she is only a girl, and will be only a woman,' he thought on. 'So, of course, no harm in particular has been done to her. But if she had been only a kitten that we had saved from drowning, we solemnly swore to do the best by her, body and life and soul, that we could; not to let her coming to grief—as of course she will—be our fault instead of her own. . . . We were bound jointly and severally, as the lawyers say. If Esdaile and Ronaine are bankrupt, and since Bassett and Urquhart repudiate, and since this fellow here does worse than either, and is not fit to bring up a sparrow, on whom does the debt fall? On me. There's no getting out of that, anyhow, twist it and look at it whichever way I will. There's only one possible thing to be done.

But how? How can I, at my age, and with my ways, saddle myself with the life of a girl? Why, I couldn't even meddle in the matter without scandal—though nobody knows me, and I should say that nobody that matters a straw knows her. But then, what have I to do with scandal, or scandal with me? Here's something that must be done by some one, if only out of common honour, and there's nobody but me to do it; and——'

'I quite agree with your sentiments,' interrupted the admiral. 'They are such that do any man honour. I always say myself that all expenses to which a fellow-man is put in the execution of his duty should be punctually repaid. It's not the money; but it's the principle of the thing.'

The admiral did not speak at all fiercely this time, but very gently and deferentially, merely saving his visitor the trouble of having to complete his own sentence, as it were.

'Of course, of course,' said Doyle hastily. 'I never knew anybody who didn't call money "the principle of the thing." They muddle the spelling a little, I suppose. So that is the girl. And so she has nobody in the place of a mother, or of a sister—nobody about her in the shape of womankind ? '

Phœbe herself began to disbelieve in the voice of nature ; or was the stranger only her grandfather, and does the voice of nature apply to grandfathers ? He did not even appear to be taking any personal notice of her, but to be speaking of her as if she were a mere nonentity in her own history—a very undignified position for a conscious heroine to be placed in.

' I have been father, mother, brother, and sister to Phœbe all in one,' said the admiral solemnly. ' It has been a lofty responsibility. But it has been piously and nobly fulfilled.'

' But surely she has been to school ? She knows other girls of her own age ? '

The admiral did not answer immediately. He could not but feel that Phœbe's friends might expect her to have been sent to school. But then they might want to know the name of the schoolmistress, and that was a question more easy to ask than to answer.

' Well, not exactly to what you might go so far as to call school. But——'

' She has not been to school ? All the better. And her friends ? '

'Friends!' exclaimed the admiral with alacrity. 'Do you suppose that I, as her responsible guardian, would allow her to mix with the people about here? They are ignorant and vulgar, sir, to the backbone. I have been her friend.'

Such a speech might have roused any other man to double pity. But not Doyle.

'Strange!' he only thought. 'A girl, and without a mother, sister, teacher, schoolfellow, or girl-friend! Why, such a girl might, in truth, become what a woman never is or has been—what a woman ought to be. If I could row in the same boat as Urquhart and Bassett by breaking my word, how could I leave a girl who, thanks to fate, has escaped from women to gain no good out of such a miraculous escape from evil? She is young, away from women; her own nature cannot surely as yet have taught her any very irreparable harm. Mr. Nelson.'

'Sir.'

'I am a plain-dealing and plain-speaking sort of man, as I dare say you see.'

'And I, sir, am a ditto. There's nothing about me that isn't plain. When I say ditto, I mean ditto; nothing less, nothing more.'

'Then I need say but few words. I have learned all that I need to know. That she has formed no ties except with yourself, and——' He had to beat about the bush; for it was needful that he himself should invent a romance off-hand, and his imagination, despite his having once upon a time been a hanger-on upon the skirts of literature, was neither so strong nor so quick as Phœbe's. 'I said that I had undertaken to make inquiries about her on behalf of her friends and family, who have come to hear of the story of her loss—no matter how; and, as I am satisfied, so will they also be. You have not asked me anything about them, nor who they are. I will tell you all that you need know.'

He was addressing vacancy, or the ceiling, as most people do who are inventing their facts as they go along. But his eyes fell, for a moment, indirectly upon Phœbe's listening face, and the sight of it inspired him, professed woman-scorner as he was, with the excitement of a new feeling that this girl was, after all, the only thing that stood to him for a phantom likeness of the purposes that other men live for, and of what they expect to find waiting for them when they come home. Had she been the plainest and commonest-looking of all womankind, he felt, there was something in his long-silent heart that was hungering for some of the links, for any of them, that bind a man to his kind. Honour and duty were at the summit of the wave; but who can guess from what distance, or from what depth, a wave may come? Certainly not he.

'There was once, I am not going to tell you how or when, since my story is not my own, a man of—of good rank and position who secretly married against his father's—and her father's—will a girl, who—well, let it be enough that she was all they say a woman ought to be, except rich——'

'Ah!' interrupted the admiral; 'that was sad, to be sure. But then it is odd that her parent should have objected to the young man.'

'They had their reasons, I suppose. Perhaps they were of those eccentric people who —I assure you I have known actual cases, strange as you may think it—who fancy that there are more important things than money; the young man may have been wild, or a gambler, or—who can tell? Anyhow, they

married without leave, and then the young
man's father, on whom he depended, quarrelled with him and cast him off, and he had
to go abroad to make a living. What was
worse for him, he had to leave his wife in
poor lodgings in London, alone. Time went
by. And—and—and when—of course you
understand that letters had ceased—when he
came home again it was to find that his wife
was dead, and that his child had been lost in
the streets of London. It had been sent out
with a nurse-girl who had never returned.
Everywhere he made inquiries—of the police,
at the workhouses, in the hospitals,' he went
on, his imagination warming as he felt •his
story working itself together without any too
apparent flaw, ' and nowhere could he obtain
a clue, until he was obliged to give up his
search in despair. But at last, by a curious
chain of circumstances, he came to learn, from
one who knew all about it at the time, your
story of the lost child. Date, even to the
hour, descriptions, all possible circumstances
agreed. He inquired yet more closely, and
to such good purpose that my own final inquiries to-night will leave not the faintest
shadow of a doubt upon my—upon my friend's

mind that his lost daughter has been found. But there are family reasons why secrecy as to all this past history should still be observed, and—and—why it should not be supposed that his daughter has ever been brought up in a manner unbecoming her position and—and—name. And therefore, to come to the point, will you, Mr. Nelson, besides having the pleasure of restoring your foster-child to her friends—will you undertake to breathe no word of anything you know or have ever known about Miss Burden? Will you separate yourself from her as if you had never known her? Will you consider Jane Burden —whatever her name was—as dead, and keep from all attempts to see her, or to learn her name? If so, you shall not lose; you shall have what, as you truly say, every Englishman expects—that his duty shall be well paid. You have, you say, hitherto done your duty —piously and nobly—for nothing. You shall henceforth do it yet more nobly—you shall do it for the arrears of that hundred a year for her bringing up that you tell me you have never received. . . . Yes,' he thought to himself, 'that has to be done too. Since they have done nothing, I must do all.'

Phœbe's ears were still busy in trying to carry all she could gather of this, to say the least of it, meagre history of her birth to her mind. It was not strange to her, for she had read of such romances over and over again. They were commoner than blackberries in the land where the leaves and blossoms of her withered bay-bush grew. More, there was no need at present to understand. But she, looking towards him who had hitherto been her father, and wondering, with some new awe and inconsistent alarms, about who her real new father might turn out to be, less understood the flash of real intelligence that suddenly beamed over the admiral's face—she had never seen such a thing there, or anything like it, before. But it was only for a moment—perhaps she had misread what she had seen.

'Phœbe!' he exclaimed, in a voice pitched so high as to be almost a wail, 'come to my side—to my left side, where my heart is—and tell them all if Horatio Collingwood Nelson is the man to surrender the child of that heart for a sum that—that—in short, isn't worth his taking, and with no more security than a stranger's bare word—I mean for all the gold

R

mines of Golconda, paid down ; that's what I
mean ! '

It was a speech—except for a few words
in the middle—after Phœbe's own heart ; it
was worthy, she felt, of an Associated Robespierre. What ought a true heroine to do ?
Should she not go at once to the side of the
only father she had ever known and refuse
even coronets and diamonds with scorn ? But
it was no natural impulse that called for an
answer. She did not go to his side ; and the
moment's opportunity for heroism was gone.

'I see,' said the stranger quietly. 'I forgot
the arrears of interest. That will come to a
good deal more ; but you're right. You must
have that too. It's stiff to reckon off-hand.
Suppose we say in round numbers, for arrears
and interest, two thousand guineas. As for
security for the money, you shall have a
cheque that will be duly honoured. I'll make
arrangements for that to-morrow ; and, understand, the signature will tell you nothing, and
any inquiries you make at the bank it is
drawn on will tell you nothing more. As for
security for getting the cheque, seeing that
Miss Burden leaves this house with me in an
hour, and without leaving an address, consider

that a father is not bound to pay a penny for the recovery of his child. Take a fair and just offer, or leave it; in offering it, my duty is done, and I shall advise him accordingly. No. I know what you are going to say. The father will not appear to claim his daughter in person. He will act wholly through me.'

Again—though Doyle saw nothing of it— the look came into the admiral's face that would make a stranger, who only saw him for these passing moments, take him for any- thing but the fool that most people thought him. And yet that look did not prevent him from saying, as simply as if Doyle had not been making him an offer which—as being without a single grain of real security, and based on no sort of sufficient proof—nobody but the most confiding of mortals could be asked to accept or even consider :

'Phœbe! Duty is duty after all. I have been a good father to you, but Heaven forbid that I should allow you to stand in my way— I mean, that I should allow myself to stand in yours—for the sake of a few paltry thousand pounds. You know I have never cared to be rich, but then there is the cause, the cause of mankind. Be a heroine, Phœbe. It is hard, my poor girl. But tear yourself away, don't cry, think of Mankind ! '

' Go ? ' asked Phœbe. ' With this—this gentleman ? Now ? And—and—what shall I do about my things ? And—who is my father ? Where is he ? Ah ! ' she cried, struck by a sudden light ; ' my father—it is you ! And—and,' she added sadly, ' if you are not, nobody is—though you don't seem like one ; you have not—taken money to send me away.'

It was not the least like the scene she had planned. It had all gone wrong. There had been no voice of nature ; no agonies at parting ; no raptures at meeting. Only a cold instinct that the Grand President of Robespierres was something of an impostor, and that story-books are something of impostors, too. Nevertheless, her broken words did not sound cold. To Doyle, they seemed to ring of something real at last ; and ' My father—it is you ! ' went more deeply through him than he could tell, and struck a chord in him that was sadly strange and sweetly new.

' Your father ? ' said he. ' Let it be so, then. . . . I did not mean to say so now. . . . But—I am he. You have no other ; and—'

never mind what you call your "things."
Get ready anyhow, and come. Come—home.'

It was the least he could say, and yet,
little as it was, it was the most, too. And,
though little was the most, there was something in its tone, for all its coldness, that
seemed to call her as if he needed her, and
to make her able to answer him in only one
way.

And thus it happened that Marion Burden
had died, and that Phœbe Doyle, the only
child of a rich English-Indian, had come into
the world. Only Stanislas Adrianski, who
had missed his plighted bride from her garden
for many wondering days, had been permitted
to recognise, amazed, the ghost of his Phœbe
in a fine lady sitting in a box at ' Olga.' And
what should he be to Phœbe Doyle? Only a
fiddler now—or a hero for ever, whatever else
he might be?

Only one thing is certain: nobody as yet,
not even herself, had ever known the real
Phœbe, with those eyes of hers that had so
wild a way of seeing all things in all forms
and colours except their own.

# PART III

*MISS DOYLE*

## CHAPTER I

### JACK DOYLE'S GHOST

THERE comes a period at least once in every life when we are compelled, whether we wish it or not, to pause and to take stock of ourselves and our surroundings, unless we are content to let ourselves and them drift into hopeless confusion. We have been hitherto obliged to regard the history of Phœbe and of so many of her fathers as do not appear to be hopelessly lost, piecemeal; following out their fortunes, now with the eyes of a girl who had learned to see all things wrongly, and then, again, with those of a man who, if he saw anything rightly, had not the art of looking round things, or of imagining that anything he saw could possibly have an unseen side.

As for the admiral, it is plain that his spectacles
can be of no value to anybody who has nothing
to sell, while Sir Charles Bassett and his old
friend had their reasons for being blind, and
the new generation of young men had no
reason for caring about chance scraps of other
people's lives. I cannot help feeling the need
of mounting a little higher above the ground
over which these people were walking without
seeing more than a yard of mist before them,
so as to take more of a bird's view of the plan
of the paths that now begin so singularly to
converge and blend. Phœbe, all unconscious
of anything that happened beyond the four
walls of an empty backyard, had been, from
her babyhood, the means of transmuting a
Bohemian of Bohemians into a sober and
successful money-lender—unless report, which
can hardly be deceived in such a case, did him
too much right or too much wrong. Who
was she? Nobody could really tell her that;
certainly not the man who, thinking himself
compelled by duty to obey the instincts of
heart-hunger—a craving from which there is
no reason to think money-lenders more free
than money-borrowers—had given her the
place in his life which, when empty and before

it hardens and closes up for ever, cries out
for the love of friend, wife, or child, wherewith
to be at least a little filled. The act of adop-
tion was sudden; but it grew as naturally out
of his life as interest from principal. He must
have been somebody even before those now
far back days when he was Jack Doyle of
the back slums; and when a man goes so
thoroughly to the dogs, one may safely guess
that he has rather more heart than his neighbours. The dogs are not fond of hearts that
are colder than brains, and had rejected him
ever since he had taken to make money.
There was nobody who cared for him. That,
perhaps, is too common to signify; but it did
signify that there was nobody for whom he
cared. He had sworn joint fatherhood to
Phœbe, to the extent of some twenty pounds
a year—a trifle, but his vow had made him
what he was—and he was the only one who
had kept it; a good reason to make him go
on keeping it, if only out of pique and pride,
to prove, perhaps, that a usurer is as good as
a baronet and may be better. In effect, he
was proud, angry, disappointed, hungry, and
alone. And so—to the admiral's exceeding
bewilderment—he had assumed the character

of the one, true, lawful, and natural father of Phœbe Burden.

For it must not be supposed that the admiral—who deserves a passing glance from our height of prospect—swallowed such a monstrous story as that a man, though twenty times a father, should come back from India to bother himself with a daughter whom he had never seen, and should pay a stranger over two thousand pounds for silence, unless silence were a very important thing indeed. He was by no means such a fool as not to argue, ' True, a promise is no security that he won't carry off the girl and leave me to whistle for my money. He gives me neither address nor name to trace him by. But then, why want the girl at all? He either is her father or else he isn't her father. If he is her father, he needn't have offered me a penny. He could have claimed her and proved his claim, and taken her off straight away. And so, being her father, there's something he wants over and above the girl that's better worth buying. And he'll buy, or else he's as sure I shall talk as that I stand here. And, if he's not her father, all the more reason why he should pay. He can't think me such an ass that I

couldn't find out what he doesn't choose to
tell. That girl worth offering two thousand
for? Then she's worth paying four thousand
for. Nothing venture, nothing win. I needn't
give up that five pound a quarter from Doyle.
And if anybody else asks after her? That
isn't likely though, now; and if they do, why
it's easy to make her as dead as a door-nail.
. . . And the boys? It's a good job Phil's
gone. It won't do, though, to tell them
about that two thousand—or three—or four.
There wouldn't be much left at the end of a
year. Let me see. . . . And I mustn't tell
them she found a rich father, or they'd be
down on him. . . . I wish I could think of a
tale for the boys. Let me see. It won't do
merely to say that she went out for milk, or
candles, and never came home. That might
strike them as queer. What would a girl be
likely to do? Put yourself in her place—
what should I have done if I'd been a girl?
I should have been sorry to part with me, of
course, but I couldn't have gone on living
with the boys. I should have gone on the
stage. But then that would be a fine excuse
for the boys to go to all the theatres in
London. No; I should have gone off with

somebody, with a young man. By Jingo!
that's the very thing. And it's true, too—all
but the young man. She made believe to go
out on an errand—no; when I came back I
found she'd gone, and left a note to say she
was very sorry and hoped we'd forgive her,
and she wouldn't do it any more, but she'd
gone off with the man of her heart to be
married (naming no names), and—yes, she's
the very girl that would do that sort of thing.
And the note? Oh, I can tear that up in a
rage. It'll break my heart, I'll never forgive
her, and forbid them ever to name her name.
And Phil? Ah, Phil! it is a good job he's
out of the way just now.'

So, changed even to her Christian name,
dead to Sir Charles Bassett, romanced away
out of the vision of her foster-brothers, effi-
ciently bought from her guardian, there was
no reason why Marion Burden, changed into
Phœbe Doyle, should ever be heard of again;
while nothing was more natural than that
there should be a Phœbe Doyle. Who was
she? It would take a clever detective to
discover that now. He would have to connect
Phœbe Doyle with Marion Burden, and Marion
Burden with some unknown child who had

been lost in its cradle days and had never
been looked for.    And the secret was less
likely to be found out inasmuch as, except to
herself, the solution was of no consequence to
a soul, while Phœbe did not dream of ques-
tioning the solution she had received.    Why
should she?    Doyle's impromptu romance of
her birth and parentage, though lame enough
to the secret mind of the admiral, was real
enough to her.    She was Jack Doyle's
Daughter, and as such her grown-up history
begins.

She afterwards remembered, with shame
for such transgression of the first laws of
the literature from which she had obtained
her knowledge of the world, that Stanislas
Adrianski had not entered her mind from
the moment when she first knew that she
saw her father to that when she found herself
beside her new-found father in a cab—a mere
common cab, and not a chariot and four.
Indeed, she had unlimited reasons for being
vexed and disappointed with herself, as soon
as the first whirl was over.    The sudden
wrench from all the early associations which
ought to have become part of her very being

had not cost her a single pang. She had forgotten to shed a single tear, while hurrying
on her bonnet, for one of the boys, though
she perfectly understood that she was never
to see one of them any more. She had not
felt faint, or resolute, or tender, or anything
that became so grand an opportunity for
bringing out the behaviour of a heroine. It
was really disappointing to find that she had
spent years in cultivating herself to this very
end, only to throw away the chance when it
came. It was too late to know now what she
ought to have said and done. Never, so long
as she lived, could she hope to be claimed by
another long-lost father. But this was all
nothing to her love treason. It had been
impossible, of course, to proclaim her engagement to Stanislas then and there. But she
might at least have scribbled a note to her
lover, wrapped it round anything heavy
enough that came to hand, and thrown it out
of a back window into his garden. She could
even see, in the air, the very words she ought
to have used: 'The secret of my life is
revealed. Constant and true. In time you
will know all.' And yet, even while she was
reading her own unwritten message to her

lover, she was doubly troubled by a yet more shameful feeling—the consciousness that she was not even sorry for her failure to act up to her own knowledge of what romance required.

'What will he think of me?' thought she. 'What will he do? The Duke of Plantagenet, when he lost Lady Adeline, disguised himself as a groom, and got a place at the castle where she was confined, and threw the marquis who carried her off from the top of a tower. I must let him hear from me; and how can I write without saying I'll be constant and true? And that I love him? I do love him; of course I do. I must manage to feel it a little more. I'll give myself five minutes, and then I really will love Stanislas with all my heart and soul——'

'Miss Burden—Phœbe,' said her companion, breaking in upon thoughts that, as usual, could not keep themselves within the lines of reality, however wild it might be, 'I don't wonder at your asking no questions. I'm afraid you must be feeling—strange. But —you mustn't go on feeling strange with me.'

'Indeed, sir,' began Phœbe, in a tone as if she had been accused of some new sin against dramatic proprieties—'indeed, sir, but it is all so strange!'

'You must learn to call me "father," just as I must call you "Phœbe."'

It would have been natural in a father, who had so much missed his lost child and had taken so much trouble to find her again, to have made some outward and visible sign of affection. But there were no tears in his voice, which did not even tremble, and his hands made no movement towards hers.

She was glad of it, for it saved her from a great deal of trouble; and yet she could not help feeling that her father was unnaturally undemonstrative and cold. As for him— well, he could not, after all, manage to make himself her father simply by calling himself so, and he felt no temptation to use the advantage which his claim had given him over a pretty and seemingly over-docile and unassertive girl. Had she been plain, his part would have been infinitely more easy. But he simply felt awkward and constrained; the suspicion never entered his head or heart for a moment that he might possibly have been taking a hand at the old game of fire. He felt himself as safe from that as he had felt from ruin when playing to lose non-existent millions in the old Bohemian days.

'Don't you ever want to know your name?' he asked after a pause.

'Of course. Phœbe——'

'You are Phœbe Doyle. My name is John Doyle. I suppose you won't be sorry to know that I am what most people call rich, and you are my only child.'

A brilliant speech came into her mind. Something to justify her character of heroine she must say or do.

'Am I like my mother?' she asked. 'Have I her eyes?'

He could not help opening his a little. It was not at the untimeliness of such a question in a dark cab, where faces could only be seen by flashes when they happened to be passing a gas-lamp; but it seemed to betray a theatrical touch about the girl that did not please him. He had noticed her eyes, and his ingrained ideas of women as a sex were strong enough to make him fancy that she knew her own strong point, and wanted a compliment, after the manner of girls who are brought up among such surroundings as hers must have been.

'Your mother?   No.'

Not even then, to her extreme wonder, did the tone of his voice change.   She had only thought of doing justice to the finer part of her own nature, and not of moving him, when she asked her question; but surely the mention of the wife whom he had loved so much by her newly-found child should have moved him deeply.

'I wonder if I should have loved my mother?' she thought sadly.   'I wonder if I can love anybody—except Stanislas, of course? I wonder if my mother loved my father?   He seems made of stone.   And I—do I take after him, that I don't seem able to feel anything at all?'

Doyle, too, fell back into silence, and it was really to think of Phœbe's mother—of that mother who had not only never died, but who had never even been born.

It was natural, after all, that her child should speak of her.   But what was he to say?   He had committed himself to saying that she was not like Phœbe.   Well, he could make her like or unlike anything he pleased; and then he thought——

If our bird's-eye view has not yet been

high enough to see back into the pre-Bohemian days of John Doyle, it was because they had been dead and buried, even so long ago as when there was a Charley Bassett, of Gray's Inn, instead of a Sir Charles Bassett, of Cautleigh Hall. Some ghosts men are able to lay out of their own sight, and therefore from the sight of all men; but what ghost is laid always and for ever? Not such a ghost as had once been slept and drunk out of sight —a spirit exorcised by spirits—by the Jack Doyle of old.

Phœbe, whether we can believe it or no, was the first girl, presumably pure and innocent, with whom, for a number of years equivalent to a lifetime, he had spoken more than a chance word. Even in his roughest and worst times he had been a notorious woman-hater, and had taken no share in what used to pass for adventures and *bonnes fortunes* among Charley Bassett and his friends. It had been a matter of chaff among them— behind his back, at least; for upon that one point it had always been dangerous to rally him openly.

But there had been—who can have for a moment doubted it?—a cause. The cause was truly not only dead, but buried, as deep underground as the corpses of the past can be laid and buried by hands of men.

But—no need to say why—the fingers of women are stronger than the hands of men. It was not Phœbe's chance question about a woman who had never been, but Phœbe's mere being in the world, and the sound of her voice so close to his ear, and the immediate nearness of her life to his own, that had called up Jack Doyle's ghost to life again. If we have not caught sight of it before, it was because it had been too completely and successfully buried to be seen.

It was as long ago as when he was a scholar of his college at Oxford—a place where, to the belief of his comrades in Bohemia, he had never been any more than they had been there themselves ; for it might have been noticed that he chose his comrades from a strictly non-collegiate circle—that the shadow of his life began. There were men about in London who would have remembered him well had he allowed them to do so ; but his holding himself out of their ken was hardly needful to save from recognition, in Jack Doyle, the student who was reading for a Fellowship to be followed by holy orders. The sermons that he had written for the price of a bout of brandy he had once meant to preach from the pulpit, and the nickname of archdeacon, which had managed to follow him even to India, was a burlesque upon what might have been a very probable reality. The worst of him at Oxford was that he was so painfully steady a young man. He was more blameless than a young Quakeress, and seemed in as little danger of coming to any sort of grief as if he had been a monk of Mount Athos, where not even so much as a hen-bird is allowed to come. But, I suppose, the rule of the monks is no rule for the air, and that at least a hen-sparrow will chance to perch upon their hardest rocks now and then. And so his doom came.

It was with an actress—of all people in the world—with an actress at a country theatre, that he fell in love, not in any common way, but to the full extreme of unknown and untried passion. He was spending his last long vacation in reading at Helmforth, the little sea-side town where, by chance, he first met the girl. Of her there is nothing else to be known; she is only visible to his eyes, and to all others dead and forgotten. The most inveterate playgoer may search in vain for the name of Miss Stella Fitzjames in his memory of the stage. He loved her so much that he made her a goddess, and did not even know that he was a fool. He did not read. He spent all he had to spend upon her, and more. He allowed himself to lose the class at which he had been aiming ever since he was a schoolboy. He cut himself off from a Fellowship that would mean celibacy. He gave up the calling for which he had unfitted himself as much as a man can.

Stella became his one thought, his complete faith, his whole world. He made no secret of his love ; he brought himself to part from her in order that he might make a clean breast of it to his friends at home. He had already bought the marriage license, and had left it in her hands. When he came back, after a hopeless rupture with his family, to Helmforth, it was to find that the license had already been used, and that, in the marriage register, there stood recorded his own name as that of the husband of Stella Fitzjames.

Who had supplanted him, and why in

such a way, he did not care to know. It
was enough, and more than enough, that his
faith in Stella's sex had been destroyed, and
that nothing, save death in life, had been
given him in return.

No wonder he shuddered a little at Phœbe's
theatrical question—

'Am I like my mother?  Have I her
eyes?'

It was as if the ghost of Stella had suddenly laid a finger on his arm.

'She shall have had no mother!' his
thoughts exclaimed. 'She shall be good and
true—she shall be like no other woman that
has ever been. Phœbe——'

At last he held out his hand. She could
not refuse hers, and he kissed it, but as little
like a father as a lover. After all, it was she
who had saved him from his worst and most
desperate self—this child. He owed her more
than two thousand pounds! In the midst of
her wonder at suddenly feeling his lips upon
her hand, the cab stopped—she did not know
in what part of the town—at the door of an
hotel.

## CHAPTER II

### THE FIRST DAYS

THAT inn door at which the cab stopped was
no common inn door. For well nigh the
first time in Phœbe's life something seemed just
what it really was. She knew it to be the
gate of the real world, outside which she had
stood and waited so long for something to
happen. That she believed the real world to
be a reflection of cheap romance has nothing
to do with the matter; the door was not the
less a real door for happening to lead into
nothing better than a common coffee-room,
instead of among people whom one could tell
at a glance to be heroes and heroines.

How her father managed to disarm the
natural curiosity of the manager of the hotel
as to the sudden arrival of a young woman,
not too well dressed, and with no luggage
worth mentioning, was a detail of business
that did not come in her way. She had been

running out of one mood into another for hours past; and her present mood was that, although it was, of course, a proud delight to have turned out a real lady, even without the additional salt of a title, still it would be a relief to wake up and find herself in her own bed at home. Home had never felt like home before. Happily for her self-respect, she never guessed the real cause of this new experience. She had eaten nothing to speak of since breakfast, and had come away without her tea.

In one thing, however, men, stupid they may be in general, are seldom quite so stupid as to forget that women cannot live by tea alone. He himself, late as it now was, had not dined, and was perfectly able to see a ghost now and then without losing his appetite. It seemed to Phœbe that the meal was a gorgeous banquet—as indeed it was, after those slipshod meals of home, for which she had herself been only too answerable. It made her feel shy; but even shyness failed to conquer healthy hunger. Her father seemed shy too; but she was too tired out with noticing things to notice any more, and the meal passed in silence which did not

prove the usual awkward burden. In short
Phœbe ate a very good dinner, and felt very
much better when she had done. I would
have said so at once; but it is not a nice thing
to say of a professed heroine, who, at such an
accusation, must have felt compelled to lay
down her knife and fork and go to bed
hungry. For here was she, eating with a
good appetite, though she scarcely yet knew
her own name; though she was torn from
the home of her childhood; and though her
lover must, if he had the heart to smoke at
all, be smoking the cigarette of suspense and
anxiety too terrible to be borne.

'I suppose,' said her father at last, 'you
must be wanting to know what sort of a life
ours is to be. I hear you have made no
friends or connections of your own—that's
well; better than I could have hoped for.
What your—what people call education—
has been I don't care a straw. The less a
woman or a man has of that stuff, the better
for her and him. Nor do I care another
straw whether you're a good housekeeper.
I want a daughter—neither a cook nor a
chambermaid. I don't care for many comforts; and those I want I can hire or buy.

I'm going to take lodgings while I look out
for a house. I've made up my mind to take
a house somewhere in London; for I sha'n't
go back to India, and one can sleep better in
London than anywhere in the world, and be
less bothered with people. Of course, you
won't want balls and parties, or any of that
nonsense, as you've never been used to them;
and I'm glad to say I've got no more acquaintances than you. I think—I hope, Phœbe,
we shall get on very well. Only one thing
you must promise me. If any of the Nelsons
try to communicate with you, in any sort of
way, or see you, or if you see them, let me
know it instantly.'

Her latest mood, thanks to satisfied hunger, had been almost rose-coloured. But a
blank fell over the tint of promise at the
words which opened out such a vista of
nothingness to a girl of quick instincts, if of
nothing more. What was the good of suddenly finding herself something like what she
had always expected if she was to make no
friends and never go to a ball? That was
not life—so much of the truth even her
romances had been able to teach her. Why,
when she used to picture herself as a princess,

it had always been as a brilliant, dancing
princess, with partners sighing round her;
never as a royal nun.   She might just as well
have been left alone with her bay-tree.

'Yes,' she said doubtfully.   'No, I have
never seen a ball.'

'And you mean to say you would like
to?' asked her father, with a rather quick
frown, considering his slow and heavy ways.

It frightened her for a moment, for it
reminded her of Phil, also slow and heavy, and
with uncomfortable views about the lives of
girls.

'Oh no, I don't mean that, of course,' she
said weakly; 'only what am I to do with
myself all day long?'

'Do with yourself?' he asked, a little
puzzled; 'oh, there's always something to do.
What have you always done?   Come, I ought
to know something about my own daughter.'

'Nothing; I've never done anything,' said
she, with a slight flush, however; for was it
nothing to have engaged herself only yesterday to Stanislas Adrianski?   'I mean, only
darned the boys' stockings, and walked in
the garden, and got breakfast and tea.'

'Nothing more?'

'Nothing, only I've read a great deal.'

'Oh, then, you have read, have you; and what books? I shouldn't have thought the admiral kept much of a library.'

'No, but they kept one just round the corner. I've read all the books they've got, nearly. I've read "Lady Ethyline," and "Denzil Wargrave; or, the Mystery of Mordred Mill," and Thad——'

She stopped; that ground was too near the estate in her heart of Stanislas Adrianski.

'I mean——'

'"Thaddeus of Warsaw." Well?'

'And "The Haunted Grange," one of the best of all.'

But she stopped again, and not unwillingly, for this uncomfortable father of hers was listening no more. And she would have been amazed indeed could she have seen into his mind just then, and read there that this big, stern, cold man, who talked as a matter of course of shutting up his only child in a hopeless nunnery of one, had himself written that thrilling, nay, gushing, romance of "The Haunted Grange," by way of desperate hackwork, in a garret, for not quite a farthing a line.

'You—has any living creature read "The Haunted Grange"?' asked he. 'Then you have read the most idiotic drivel that ever was penned. And I suppose the others are much the same. Well, we can change that, anyhow. I'm glad I know.'

Doyle, as he smoked his last cheroot of the day in refreshing solitude, could not, somehow, manage to congratulate himself thus far on the prospects of the results of his impulse to adopt a daughter. He did not regret the first step of the experiment, but he felt he had played his part ill, and that Phœbe required a little more educating than he expected to become his daughter indeed. Of selfishness in the matter he had no consciousness at all. A sense of duty, as usual, served as a cloak for all other things. And yet, even as things were, he might have found cause to tell himself that he had really done—for himself, at least—well. He had somebody else to think of, and to think of somebody else with discomfort and misgiving was something to the man who had never had anybody but himself to think of since his ghost was laid. Before he slept, that ghost came back to him once more.

As for Phœbe, she fell asleep at once, and dreamed neither of father nor of lover. She dreamed of nothing at all. And so ended her first day as Jack Doyle's daughter.

It is lucky that strong impulses mean blindness to details, or they would never be followed. Whatever the temptation might have been, it is impossible to imagine for an instant that a man to whom women had become creatures of another planet would have dared to face the sight of the unknown world through which he must travel in order that he might give her the outward varnish of her new position. If possible, he knew even less of her outer requirements than of her inner needs, though, of course, he had a general idea that, leaving home in such a hurry, she must want a good many things. After turning the matter over in his mind, he could only come to the conclusion that she must get them for herself, and that all he could expect himself to do was to pay. And he had got into the habit of not being fond of paying, and called to mind the terrible stories he had heard, and, may be, known of at second hand, out in India, of milliners' bills.

'If I knew of only one woman with

daughters, I declare I'd eat my own principles, and ask her to help me,' thought he. 'I suppose Mrs. Urquhart isn't worse than other men's wives; and she'd be priceless just now. She'd combine experience with economy. I wonder if she'd show me the door again, if I let her know I'm not the poor devil she took me for, with designs on her husband's purse and morals. However, it's too late for Mrs. Urquhart now. I wonder if men think of the chances of daughters when they marry. Not, I should say.'

The result was that Phœbe, who had hitherto been clothed like the lilies, in so far as she did not know how, but very unlike them in the matters of taste and sufficiency, found herself under general orders to go to any shop she liked, and to buy whatever she wanted in the way of bonnets and gowns (so he profanely called what women wear), and all toilette trappings, so long as she left jewellery alone. He knew he was running a terrible financial risk, but his ignorance was too profound for giving her any sort of advice with detail, and he could only comfort himself with the reflection, 'In for a penny, in for a pound—she'd better get her whole outfit

once for all, and have done.' But he need
not have been afraid. With all the best will
to clothe herself gorgeously, Phœbe felt like
a little boy who, for the first time in his
life, is taken into a pastrycook's by some
rashly generous patron, and ordered: 'There
—eat as much as you can of everything you
like that you see.' The difficulty is not in
want of appetite, but in knowing how and
where to begin; so that he becomes credited
with a temperance and modesty beyond his
years and nature. Phœbe's one practical idea
was the draper's where she had been in the
habit of dealing, and of leaving anybody who
liked—who had liked had been poor Phil's
secret—to pay. But she knew that the
draper's shop would not do any more, and ye
could not think of grander shops without an
almost religious awe. She had often looked
through windows, but with no more thought
of entering, even in her dreams, than of writing one of the books in which she read of the
people whom she saw going in. This was a
reality; and it therefore found her unprepared.

'Do you mean I must go—all by myself?'
she asked. 'I—I don't know these streets;

and I don't know what people buy—you know
we have always been very poor.'

'And so you don't want much? All the
better. Yes, shopping must be a nuisance;
but I suppose it has got to be done. By the
way, though, I have an idea. We'll find
some big place together, and I'll put you altogether into the hands of some head woman
there, and ask her to do for you. She won't
ask questions; and if she does, we needn't
answer them. Everybody will see I'm from
India, and they'll take for granted you've
come from there too; and everybody here
fancies that anything odd is natural in an
Indian. We'll do that first, and then go on a
house hunt. So be ready in half an hour.'

Doyle must really have had a long purse,
considering the manner in which, when he
fairly faced them, he managed to make the
smaller wheels of life go as if they were well
oiled. At first Phœbe had really no time to
feel herself alone, or the hours empty, seeing how well the lady who undertook to do
for her professionally contrived to fill them.
What the latter thought is no matter. Middle-
aged gentlemen do now and then have daughters whose outfit for life, owing to various

circumstances, has been too long neglected, and who show signs of having had a mother of social position inferior to the father's. And, for that matter, Phœbe, in spite of every adverse circumstance, had not acquired any of the tricks of speech or manner by which a *modiste* knows better than anyone else to distinguish a 'young person' from a lady. There was more about Phœbe than her face that went towards fitting her for the stage.

Phœbe had even failed to find the time for writing that note to Stanislas, and the duty kept putting it off so constantly, and the period of neglect had grown to seem so much longer than it really was, that it became daily doubly difficult to do. When she had been dressing, and her father house-hunting, for a week that seemed as full as ten, she had reached the stage when something that has been delayed so long can just as well be delayed another day without signifying. She did once write half the note, but she could not please herself, and tore it up again, carefully burning the remains in a candle. The fragment had been disgracefully cold; and so, perhaps, she thought that it wanted warming.

Though father and daughter were as far

from knowing one another as ever, still they
had become better acquaintances, if not better
friends.   When shyness sinks very deep, it
often becomes invisible.   Neither had got
what he or she had wanted.   But Phœbe was
too busy to miss anything as yet, and had her
entanglement on her mind ; and Doyle thought
himself engaged in a study of the character
which he had determined, now that he had
apparently given up all other business, to
form.   So one day, when the dressing business was nearly over, he said :

'I don't know what sort of things you like
best yet, Phœbe.   It can't be books, because
nobody could care for that trash you told me
of, except born fools.   You've never learned
a note of music, thank goodness, and I can't
make out that you've got any tastes at all.   I
want your life to be happy.   If you could do
just what you liked for a week, what would
it be ?   Never mind what it is, only tell me
honestly, whatever it might be.'

She had ceased to stare at any of his questions by this time ; and she had also learned
that he was not to be denied a really full and
honest answer.   And, for once, about a full

and honest answer there happened to be no difficulty at all.

'I have never been to a theatre in my life,' she said, ' and I should like to see a real play, more than anything in the world.'

' A play !' He started ; it was the last thing he looked for. And Stella had been the last actress he had seen on the stage ! ' What on earth can have put that into your head, Phœbe ? A play ? '

' Oughtn't I to want to see a play ? I thought the greatest ladies went to plays, and I've always thought it would be so grand and beautiful to see all the things one thinks of, to see them with one's very eyes. It would be like living in a book—not like reading one.'

She did not often have the chance of speaking her mind out, and she was apt to lose the chance when it came. But she did not lose it now. She had always felt a dumb hunger for every sort of dreamland in which her eyes and ears might outdo her fancy ; and the prospect of real life seemed likely to prove so woefully inferior to printed dreams that her hunger had been growing for living ones.

He did not notice how unlike her usual words her last were. For once there was something like a point in them, and more than merely reflected feeling.

'A play,' said he again. 'No,' he thought, 'I have not lived so long in my own way to change it now, which means—which means I am a coward and a weak fool, who has not outlived and forgotten, and am afraid of finding out what an impostor I am. That will never do. . . . I have forgotten, and I am not afraid. What have I taken this poor child into my life for but to begin a new life, as if the past had never been? As long as I dare not face one least single memory, I have not conquered; and conquer I will. It sha'n't be put on my tombstone, "Here lies a man who was such a fool that he couldn't forget a girl, and who was afraid to go to a play for fear he should see the ghost of her ghost there." I ought, by rights, to avoid the play of life, because she was a living woman once upon a time. . . . Phœbe, I will—I mean you shall—see a play.'

# CHAPTER III

### ' ONLY A FIDDLER '

' You shall go to the play,' was spoken in the
tone of a rather angry father towards a dis-
obedient boy—as if Phœbe had already been
ordered to go to the play, and had stubbornly
refused to do any such thing. Of course it
was Doyle himself whom Doyle, in spirit, had
called 'You'; it was one of his two selves
addressing the other. But it all came practically to the same thing. His tone of command
was, after all, more satisfactory than a mere
cold and indifferent 'Very well, then—you
may go' would have been. She had never
yet been commanded or ordered about with
anything like authority, even by Phil; and
the sensation was a little piquant and not at
all disagreeable. Doyle might have fancied
himself disappointed could he have seen, in
spite of her having had to tumble up anyhow

among boys, the amount of the natural woman that there was in Phœbe.

So soon as the matter was settled, it was he, and not she, who set about this simple business of playgoing as if it were a serious affair. He did not say much about it, but any woman, without going a finger's breadth below the surface, could see that it occupied his thoughts quite as much as house-hunting. Phœbe, as we know, was something of a clairvoyant in her way, and though, like clairvoyants in general, she nearly always saw either wrongly or else what was not to be seen at all, she could not, when things lay very much on the surface, help seeing more or less rightly now and then. But it did not strike her that there was anything like a childish streak in this part of her father's behaviour. On the contrary, unsympathetic as its manifestations were, it made her feel that plays are a more really important part of life even than she had supposed.

She was spared that half-hour of agony during which playgoers, in the first stage of their career, become quite convinced that the inconceivably indifferent middle-aged or elderly relation who is to take them will never

have finished drinking his last, lingering glass
of wine; that his last two inches of cigar
have grown, during the last two minutes,
longer instead of shorter; that no cab will be
found on the rank; and that, in short, the
farce will have to begin without them.
Phœbe's father proved himself a model for
playgoers of his age. He was ready to the
instant, as if he were a soldier on duty, and
yet did not grumble at having been kept
waiting by a single look or word. The cab
was not late, was not exceptionally slow, and
met with no delays; so that Phœbe's first
experience of a theatre was one of unfilled
stalls and the curtain down.

Her father, as they settled themselves in
their box, had still the air of a soldier on
duty. But it was with a sense rather of disappointment than of relief that he found
himself by no means so affected with the pain
of old memories and associations as he had
expected to be. When he had been a playgoer at Helmforth he had been under a spell,
which made that shabby little house a more
wonderful temple of mystery to him than to
the youngest child in the theatre. And it
was not the place, he remembered, but the

spell under which the place had been. Even
after the curtain rose, and 'Olga' was exercising
all the small magic of which it was capable,
the man of later middle age mentally rubbed
his eyes, and wondered whether he had
been dreaming in those days, or if he were
dreaming now. To find himself sitting, after
all these years, in a box at a theatre with a
young girl by his side was dream-like enough ;
but it was among his own once familiar ghosts
that he had been dreading to find himself
sitting, and not one of them was there. It is
a real disappointment, even to a man of the
age of reason, to find that one has been afraid
of shadows which, as soon as they are faced,
fly away, and do not even give one the
satisfaction of a battle and a victory. So it
was with Doyle. The battle-ground on which
he had resolved to make the last stroke of
conquest over his past turned out to be but
a mere empty field, in which no past was
present to be conquered. He not only did
not, but could not, see the form of Stella
floating in the vapour of the footlights, or feel
as he had once felt during the pause contrived
to give the leading lady an effective entry.
So stubborn did fancy prove, that he at last

caught himself trying to force up the ghosts of which he fancied himself afraid. Then, at last, like a wise man, he shrugged his shoulders, left off worrying the ghosts, and—more like a middle-aged man, if less like a wise one— took for granted that in so empty a place his companion found nothing more than he could find. 'There's nobody here to play Stella to her—fool,' thought he. 'I'm glad I came. I'm more of a dead man than I thought I was—and a good thing too.' But now that his heart-ache was over, he felt that it had been a sort of luxury while it lasted, after all, and he missed the pain. 'I suppose this is the first sign of growing old—the first real grey hair.'

Phœbe lost no time in throwing her heart over stalls, orchestra, and footlights right into the middle of the stage. Although the inside of a theatre was not in the least like its picture in her imagination, she felt no dis- appointment and no disillusion. Something in the very atmosphere was like the effect of native air, and made her feel, for the first time in her life, at home. Or rather it made her feel like one who goes home again after an absence of many years. The excitement she felt was not that of a mere foreign traveller who, after long visions of longed-for lakes and mountains, finds himself at last among them. What she felt was the unconscious, self-forgetful excitement of recognition; everything she saw and heard seemed to answer to a memory, like the caw of rooks and the scent of wall-flowers in the sun. Every detail, down to the smallest and most trivial, was new, and yet not one was strange. And why should an acted phantom of unreal and impossible life, like this now forgotten Olga, be strange to a girl who had been an actress all her life, with herself for dramatic author, manager, and audience, all in one? This was her real life at last, because it was the realisation of all unreality. She threw her whole self into Olga; it was not the actress for whom the part had been written that was acting, but Phœbe Doyle. And the charm of it to her was not, as to simpler minds, that it seemed like reality, but because she knew all the time that it was only a play.

So another miscomprehension of one another, never to be explained away by words, rose between Doyle and her. He saw her thorough absorption, and set it down to the natural effect upon a novice of new excitements

and new scenes, regarding it with the tolerant
pity of hearts that imagine themselves killed
at last for those that are still alive. She had
no thought for him at all, but quite understood, without the trouble of thinking, why
even so severe a father should have acted as
if it were the first duty of man and woman
to go to the play—why he had not said
' you may,' but ' you shall.' Suppose that the
hours of daylight were fated to be spent like
those of a cloistered nun—what then, if they
were to be regarded but as intervals of rest
before the Gas shed her beams over the world,
and the Curtain rolled away, and the light
which never was on sea or land, save on those
which are made of canvas and timber, arose?
I suppose Phœbe was as mere a heathen as a
savage who does not know even so much of
civilisation as the taste of its fire-water. But
who believes, like the savage, in the reality of
an ideal world? Phœbe had not only found
hers, but had seen it with her eyes.

And then, just when nothing was less in
her thoughts, her eyes turned and met the
fixed stare of Stanislas Adrianski.

No wonder she started, and turned crimson,
and wondered what such a chance could

mean, and wished—though in other words—
that the author of her romance had not made
so uncomfortable a blunder as to bring his
hero face to face with his heroine just there
and just then. The sight of Stanislas made
her conscious that the house had an audience
as well as a stage ; and her hero, with the
gas-light full upon his upturned face, did not
look so supremely fascinating as when he had
paced his back-yard in a London twilight,
and had no comparisons to fear. She knew
her sudden flush was of startled guilt towards
her neglected, and, as he had every right to
believe, forsaken, lover, and she read sternly
just upbraiding in his stony stare, and the
effects of a heart half-broken in his sallow
cheeks and melancholy length of hair. It
was as if he were pointing her out to the
whole house as a woman who, for the sake of
wealth, had thrown over the lover to whom
she had bound herself while poor and unknown,
because he was poor and unknown still. It
was not, it could not be, true ; for what could
be a greater sin? She brought her fan well
into play, taught by instinct that it had other
uses than those it was made for, and managed to glance at her father over her right

shoulder. Fortunately, he was not looking towards the orchestra just now ; but he might at any moment, and what would happen then ?

Happily he did not, or, if he did, saw nothing remarkable in a fiddler's exercise of his right to stare in any direction he liked when his eyes were off duty. But Phœbe's complete enjoyment of her first play was gone. It was a relief when Stanislas was obliged to take his part in the lively music to which the curtain next rose. But it was only a relief from the fear that something might instantly happen, as in books and plays ; the strain of the situation still remained. She left the stage, stepped into the orchestra, and put herself in the place of Stanislas Adrianski. She became now the poor, proud noble, compelled by poetical injustice to make use of his genius for daily bread while his sword was waiting for better times. She had not known, of course, that music was one of her lover's gifts, but it was quite part of the nature of things that it should be so, seeing that romance never fails to be the gainer when it obliges hero or heroine to fight ill-fortune with brush, bow, or pen. She saw his mind filled with justly indignant thoughts of her, while, by a picturesque contrast, his fingers had to bend themselves to trivial tunes that meant nothing, instead of extemporising Titanic symphonies of Love, Wrath, and Despair. She knew quite enough of music to know what the magic of romance enables its musicians, and its musicians alone, to do. Have we not known them, by sheer force of natural genius, take up a hitherto unpractised instrument, and, without a moment's thought, put the most finished performers nowhere by making it perfectly express the most delicate lights and the deepest shades of their souls' tragedies? She could hear, without the help of her everyday ears, that one particular fiddle singling itself out from the rest, and playing unwritten passages for her alone. Would it be quite impossible to ask her father for his pencil, scrawl a few words upon the back of her play-bill, fold the bill up, address it to Count Stanislas Adrianski, and let it flutter down accidentally into the orchestra? Quite impossible—although, being quite according to the rule of romance, it did not strike her as cunning or mean. Spanish ladies, she had always understood on the best

authorities, can say more with a flutter of the
fan than other women can with their tongues.
But none of her authorities had supported
their assertion by showing how it is done;
and besides, her injured lover's eyes were not
in the long black hair which—otherwise
happily—was all of him that he could turn
towards her while he was playing. That was
especially fortunate, because the musicians
have to remain at their desks throughout the
last act of ' Olga.'

Her father, without any of the awkward-
ness that his old friends would have expected
from the archdeacon when trying to do the
duties of a cavalier in waiting, helped her on
with her cloak, and was not too moved by
the ancient association of his heavy hands
with another scarlet cloak upon another pair
of shoulders to notice a bright glow upon his
daughter's face that made him pleased to
think she could so easily be made childishly
happy. Phœbe—how do all girls, as if they
were dumb creatures and free from the blindness of reason, understand all such things
without experience or teaching?—was conscious of a certain solemn tenderness in the
way in which her father covered her shoulders

before leaving the box; and it touched her
with a new sense of being protected and
cared for. What was her precise relation
to Stanislas? She wished she knew. How
would it be if, that very night, she could
conquer her growing awe for the father of
whom even yet she knew that she understood
absolutely nothing by telling him her whole
story? But there should be little need to set
out the army of instincts, doubts, shames, and
shynesses which kept a girl who had never
made a confidence since she was born recoil
from bringing herself to tell the eventless
story of a first romance to one who would
obviously prove so unsympathetic as he. She
would not have known, even, how to tell it to
a sister, if only for want of knowing how to
begin; and the language did not exist, except
in her books, wherein so shadowy a story
could be told. And then, thus far, she would
have to tell it to her own shame; and—but
one can more easily imagine a moth's taking
an elderly elephant into her confidence about
the vague attractions of a candle. Phœbe
could not quite forget how Phil had taken
the affair of Stanislas; and her father was a
great deal more awful in his deference and

tenderness than Phil had been with all his rough and jealous ill-humour.

The corridor was rather crowded, so that it took them several minutes to pass from their box to the head of the stairs. She saw Lawrence speak to her father, and heard herself, for the first time, introduced to a stranger by her full new style of Miss Phœbe Doyle. It was true that Miss Phœbe Doyle was being introduced to Mr. Lawrence. But it would be strange if she did not feel confused as to which of her many selves happened just then to be the real one, for, at the same instant, Phœbe Burden recognised the presence of Stanislas Adrianski not a dozen yards away. It is impossible to conceive any situation more completely like the confusion of a dream in which we are at the same time ourselves and not ourselves, and carry on with ease two distinct and inconsistent lives, unprepared in one of our persons for whatever may happen to us in the other. It seemed as if Phœbe Burden had nothing to do with Phœbe Doyle, and that if Phœbe Doyle confessed as her own the guilty experiences of Phœbe Burden, her confession would not be true. Of course, when thus doubled, we know perfectly well

that only one of us can be the actress, and
only one the real woman. But which is the
actress and which the real woman? Phœbe
Burden or Phœbe Doyle? Phœbe, apart
from the puzzle of surnames, was no con-
jurer, and therefore did not know. Phœbe
Doyle passed through her first introduction
to a stranger with becoming dignity. It was
Phœbe Burden whose eyes did not dare to
meet those of her lover—Phœbe Burden's
lover, and not Phœbe Doyle's at all. Why
should Phœbe Doyle tell tales of Phœbe
Burden? That would be really mean.

I do not know with how much or with
how little ease a fiddler, when his duty is
over, may transport himself into the corridors
from his unknown regions underneath the
stage. But were it ten times as hard as it
can possibly be, and though the road be
barred as high as the chin with fines and
orders, I have a certain faith in the creed that
love will find out the way from anywhere to
anywhere—at any rate if helped by hunger.
Poor and unheroic indeed were the soul of
that struggling genius who, having gained a
girl whom he thought might turn out to be
worth a little, should let her go without a

stroke so soon as he could see her to be probably worth a great deal more. What might be the relation of his Phœbe of the back-yard to the big man with the big beard who had taken her to the play in the style of a fine lady? There was nothing in the appearance of things to alarm his moral sense. Perhaps love's instinct could trust her purity; perhaps his moral sense was large and unfettered; perhaps (for heroes are privileged in such things) he had no particular moral sense at all. But, not being blind, he could read in her disorder of face and bearing, when she met his first gaze of surprise, a hundred proofs that if he chose to lose his influence over her he would be a fool. He did, after all, read, if he failed to comprehend, the language of her fan. It signalled him to her side; and, without losing a moment, he was there. 'Miss Phœbe Doyle.' It was a name which, spoken loudly and clearly, was quite easy for the most foreign of ears to catch and remember. So she was clearly a rich man's daughter, and her name was Phœbe Doyle.

Would he speak to her? thought Phœbe. Would he make a scene? Could she prevent

such a chance by any sort of warning or
imploring sign? If he had known her
through and through, he could not have
acted more wisely. He had to thank Nature
for having given him a pair of eyes that
always, and not only when they had reason,
seemed at once to appeal like a woman's and
to command like a man's. But it was a touch
of real inspiration that brought him to the
door of the cab into which Phœbe was just
about to be helped by her father. It was not
by accident—unless by one of the accidents
which never happen except to those who
know how to grasp them, and how to win by
them. He forestalled a professional copper-
hunter and opened the door, throwing upon
Phœbe a look that concentrated all tragedy
without the help of a word. How could she
have suspected so complete a gentleman of
being capable of making a scene? His
delicacy smote her with new shame. He did
not so much as raise his hat, or bow; he
only took care that her dress should not be
soiled.

'Sixteen Harland Terrace,' was reward
enough for his trouble.

'Come, out of the way, my man,' said

Doyle, who only saw a pale, patched face and a very bad hat, and was completely insensible to the signs that show nobility down at heel to be nobility still. 'Oh, you want something, I suppose, for doing nothing. There, then.'

He dropped a copper or two into what he took for the hand of a runner for cabs—not many, for he never threw away small things. To his surprise, they were scornfully tossed under the cab-wheels.

Stanislas, being poor, threw away small things freely, and not merely when they happened to be sprats to catch mackerel.

'Why, what the deuce are you?' asked Doyle, remembering the ways of Bohemia.

'I am only a fiddler,' said Stanislas, with a magnificent manner and a magnificent bow, that went to the depth of Phœbe's soul—not that the depth may be thought very far. 'Doyle, Sixteen Harland Terrace,' thought he, and then, the departing cab having left them uncovered, picked up the pence, and put them into his pocket, after all.

## CHAPTER IV

### UNCLE RAYNER AND THE OLD GREY MARE

It may, not quite impossibly, be still remembered that the succession of Charley Bassett to his baronetcy and to the family estate of Cautleigh had been both singular and unexpected. There was Sir Mordaunt Bassett— the baronet at the opening of this history— who died unmarried, and who was succeeded by his only brother, the rector of Cautleigh. But he also had found no time to marry before he died, only three weeks after Sir Mordaunt ; and so, as his short tenure had not even allowed him time to make a will, and as he left not so much as an inconvenient sister to part the land from the title, both title and estate should have fallen, in the natural course of things, to a certain uncle, one Rayner Bassett, or to the heirs of the said Rayner. This was all perfectly clear and beyond question ; and, if this had been all, Charley, whose

father had been Rayner's next and younger
brother, would have had no more chance of
becoming Sir Charles than the admiral of
becoming Sir Horatio.

But, to commit the sin of repetition for
the last time, this had—happily or unhappily
—not been all. Most families have their
black sheep, and Rayner Bassett had been the
black sheep of his from the first possible
moment after his first birthday. Whether he
was absolutely bad I do not know, and have
no means of knowing. But the weak strand
which must have been noticed from the beginning in the rope of the Bassett character,
plainly enough in Ralph, and as certainly, if
less plainly, in Sir Charles, was multiplied in
Rayner's case by ten. He had been an unlucky child; he had been an unlucky boy; he
was an unlucky man. He took up life by the
wrong end, and stuck to his hold like a bull-
dog; for he was as obstinate as only a weak
man can be. He had not even so much luck
as to be handsome, or clever, or an agreeable
companion, or to have the sort of vices the
possession of which sometimes make a man
liked the better—even his faults were all at
the wrong end. Only once in the whole course

of so much of his career as people knew did he meet with a fellow-creature who thought him worthy of a better fate than that of the dog who gets a bad name ; and the expression of the thought is worth noting for more directly important reasons than that of eccentricity. It was when he was nearly eighteen years old.

'Bassett minor,' said one of his masters to another, 'is a sneak, and a cad, and a cur. But do you suppose it's because he likes being bullied and called names? It's because he's miserably vain, and, therefore, miserably shy. I expect when he's asleep, and, may be, when he's widest awake, too, he dreams he's cock of the school. That sort of thing is wretched for a boy ; but it mayn't be so bad for him when he's out of his teens. He's the stuff poets are made of—not the big ones, but those who make a trade of breaking their hearts and selling the bits for a good round sum. It's on the cards that the fellows who now send him to Coventry will some day brag of having known him at school. But if he doesn't catch the trick of rhyming—well, if I had my way, I'd thrash him well if he didn't bring me fifty rhymes a day. I don't want to hear of his being sent to gaol for picking pockets instead

of brains. His fault is that he wants to be at
the top of the tree ; as he can't jump, he has
to crawl, and crawling isn't a graceful thing.'

This was the best thing ever said of Rayner
Bassett ; and, unluckily, the knack of rhyming
never came. He did not, on the other hand,
meet with the ill-luck of being caught with his
fingers in a pocket that was not his own ; but
he fell into the scarcely less unfortunate scrape
of presenting at one of the county banks a
cheque apparently signed by a certain most
respectable farmer, who proved most conclu-
sively that the signature was not his own. It
was a terrible affair. The then baronet, Rayner's father, did all he could to cover it, but
in vain. The farmer, an independent Briton
who paid his rent to another landlord, was
neither to be bought nor persuaded ; he stuck
to it that forgery was forgery, snapped his
fingers at the Bassetts, and swore that if the
bank shirked its duty he would do nothing of
the kind. There was nothing for it but for
Rayner Bassett to cut and run ; and the last
heard of him by his relieved relations was that
he had been living under different names, and
at different places, with a lady who was presumably his wife, and an increasing family of

small children. And then he was lost for good and all.

Of course, the precise nature of his domestic relations mattered very little at the time. But when the death, first of his father, then of his brother, then of his nephew Sir Mordaunt, then of his other nephew the rector, left the baronetcy vacant, it mattered a very great deal. If living, he, the more than suspected forger, by this time a probable gaol bird, would be Sir Rayner Bassett; which was too terrible an idea. So terrible was it as to be presumably impossible. He must be dead. Such inconvenient people as he sometimes die, if they drink enough, but, while alive, they never disappear; unless, indeed, their friends and relations are hopelessly poor. But he might, though dead, be just as inconvenient as if he were alive. There was that woman, and there were those children. Their existence had been only too certain. And was he not only their father, but had he been married to their mother? If so, though dead, he had left an heir.

To do Charley Bassett justice, he, acting under the advice of his solicitors, took all proper steps for the discovery of his missing uncle and unknown cousins. He also—as much for his own sake as for theirs—had diligent inquiry made for the fact of any possible marriage made by his uncle Rayner. It was pending the issue of these inquiries that he travelled abroad ; and not till every legal presumption was satisfied of the disappearance from life of Rayner Bassett, unmarried, did he fairly enter upon his new life at Cautleigh Hall. Nor, even then, until the legal period of possession was fulfilled, did he feel absolutely secure. The path from Bohemian to baronet was not a simple one, after all. Rank and wealth were endeared to him by danger. He took to economy as a means of hedging against some possible claim for mesne profits. He tried to make his son and heir a working-man with a view to the worst that might befall.

But the twenty years of possession were at last fairly complete, and Uncle Rayner had always been far too unlucky a man to have tumbled into idiocy, lunacy, or any other method of extending the term. Sir Charles Bassett might at last feel as secure as any man can be of anything in this uncertain world. He had never seen his uncle Rayner ; but his touch of artistic fancy had painted a very

complete picture of the scapegrace in his mind.
Of course, a family label had been pasted on
Rayner, containing his full description ; and,
of course, being a family label, it was wrong.
Feeble obstinacy in folly had been painted in
the darker colours of resolute and desperate
villainy.   Uncle Rayner was a dangerous pro-
fligate, with the physique attaching to such a
reputation ; for when a man is supposed to
have committed a murder, who does not at
once exclaim that he looks the very image of
a murderer ?   Sir Charles, as an artist, physio-
gnomist, and man of the world, was bound, by
all reason as well as instinct, to picture this
terrible Uncle Rayner as a big, burly, handsome, gentlemanlike ruffian, invincible with
women, dangerous with men ; to be avoided,
but not to be despised.   He certainly did not
picture him as a man likely to forego a great
estate out of respect for the prejudices of
Lincolnshire.   This alone had been moral, if
not legal, evidence of death—imagination is
the very grandmother of reason.

So much for the history of Rayner Bassett,
as it was known, more or less imperfectly, to
his few relations and to the still fewer whom,
as a matter of form, he might have called his

friends. The conclusion of the whole matter was that, after some twenty years and more of doubt and secret insecurity, Sir Charles Bassett might breathe freely and safely, and feel himself to be Sir Charles Bassett indeed. The character of the ex-Bohemian had hardened and stiffened ; but that only made the sensation of relief the more welcome. One must have cramped limbs to know the luxury of stretching them. He might, so far as habit would let him, relax his system of increasing his personal property by investments at the expense of the land, so that, in case he ever should turn out to have been merely a steward, he might not prove to have been a steward for nothing. The twenty years were well past and over now, and the security which duly followed relief had been growing day by day, until the old anxiety was as practically forgotten as the toothache of yesterday. It was not always that he would have written so light a letter to his son on the latter's aimlessness and idle ways ; but then, there was no longer the same need that Ralph should be able, in case of need, to open the oyster of life with a sword instead of a silver spoon. Then there was the land absolutely crying out for

all kinds of improvements which had been
neglected by an owner who could not feel
sure, till now, that what he had was his
own. The Bassetts of the direct line had
been such old-fashioned people, and of such
little enterprise, that a considerable portion of
the Lincolnshire estate was still mere un-
drained marsh and fen. Sir Charles himself
was not a particularly energetic or practical
person, but his first instinct was to commit
some act of unquestioned and unquestionable
ownership, and the most obvious act was to
set about draining and reclaiming the waste of
Cautleigh Holms. There was a certain large-
ness, too, about the notion that promised good
room for his life to stretch in ; just as, when a
young man, he had always liked his canvases
to be at least twice as large as his ideas. He
had just reached the point of life when the
Indian summer of second youth is apt to
begin, wherein those who can catch the season do their largest and their best, just before
it grows too late to begin anything new.

So, after turning the matter over in his
mind for a few months, he made up his mind
in a single hour, and, full of a second birth of
zeal, set off that very morning to London, to

lay his plans before a well-known firm of
engineers. An arrangement for somebody
belonging to the firm to come down and look
over the Holms was soon made; and Sir
Charles was at leisure, well before dinner-
time, to call at Urquhart's chambers in the
hope of finding his son there. But Urquhart
was still away at his great arbitration case in
the North, and Ralph, so he learned, had not
been at chambers that day. And, on going
to his lodgings, he further learned that Mr.
Bassett had gone out an hour ago and was not
likely to be back till some time unknown.
It was irritating; and the whole thing looked
erratic and unsteady to the ex-Bohemian. He
had not planned a lonely evening, and had
looked forward, with a newly-awakened desire
for confidences and sympathies, to telling
Ralph all about the Holms scheme. The heir
might even catch some of the improvement
fever; and that would be a grand thing—
better even than a dose of Quarter Sessions as
a training for the future squire of Cautleigh.
He did not feel inclined to dine at his club
with himself for his only guest, and a dinner
at his hotel would be worse still. And so it
came to pass that a very strange adventure

happened to him ; stranger than may seem
likely to those who are unable to read between
the lines of lives.

His mind was running on the Holms, and
this made him a little absent-minded. He
was going nowhither in particular, and yet
he was bound to arrive somewhere. He was
the most respectable of baronets, and yet
certain old instincts had been faintly revived.
And so the chain of those old instincts, with
every link an old association, drew him east-
ward until the daylight imperceptibly grew
into gas-light, and he found himself at the
narrow door of a dark passage within Temple
Bar—that gate of a million memories which
the story-tellers of the future will have to
describe with cold pens, instead of merely
naming it, as we may do still, with the re-
spectful silence that, for so many of us, its
manifold associations with our own lives make
its due.

Charley Bassett—not Sir Charles—had
once known that passage well. He had
known it as a schoolboy knows every inch of
the old school bounds, so that, twenty years
after, he can find his way to any corner of
them blindfold. For up that court was the

Old Grey Mare. The Old Grey Mare went
the way that all things go for which anybody
cares before Temple Bar; but there are men
—some rich, more poor—who remember that
very dirty den as their school, college, home
—as everything that one house can be to
one man. To the profane eye, it was simply
a singularly unattractive chop-house, which
nobody would enter except for a wager. But
nowhere round Bow Bells had the midnight
chimes been heard to sound so merrily;
nowhere had headaches been more genially
earned. There had been brave nights at the
Old Grey Mare twenty, and forty, aye, and
sixty years ago, when men were not compelled
to keep their good things for their printers,
but let them out freely upon all comers, and
when licensed hours were unknown. It had
been a house of talk, where a few famous men
had drawn their first blood as wits, and where
beaten men had been content, and more than
content, to win all their laurels. And there,
in what were now the old times, had Charley
Bassett, with his pleasant ways and his four
hundred a year, once been a greater man than
was Sir Charles in Lincolnshire. In Lincoln-

shire he was a great landlord. But he had
been a great musician, a great painter, a great
poet, and a great good fellow at the Old Grey
Mare.

What did Shakespeare do when, settled
down respectably at Stratford, he came up to
town and chanced to find himself standing
before the sign of the Mermaid? Certainly he
went in. Even Sir Charles was not without
the touch of human nature which makes the
common acts of great men and small men very
much the same. Sir Charles Bassett would
not have asked his son Ralph to take a chop
with him at the Mare; indeed, a year or two
ago he would himself, though without a companion, have passed by without a thought of
entering. But now—well, he might do as he
pleased, and there was nobody to wonder at
his choosing such a place for a meal. Charley
could not be quite killed by having been
turned into Sir Charles, and so all that remained of him yielded to natural impulse,
broke through the shell of twenty years, and
just because there was it and there was he—
he turned up the court and entered the
Mare.

Any Lincolnshire neighbour would have

suspected some mystery on seeing Sir Charles
Bassett, of Cautleigh Hall, forsake the comfort
of his club for a hole like this, to which no
mere chance could possibly have led him.
And the discovery that there was no mystery
at all about the matter would not have disappointed the neighbour more than the atmosphere of the Old Grey Mare disappointed Sir
Charles. The place was not the same. It is
true that the sawdust-carpet appeared to have
never been renewed since he had last dined
there, and that the same clock ticked, and that
the arrangement of the boxes and their tables
was precisely the same as of old. But the
room itself seemed to have shrunk into half
its former size, and the ghosts of past meals had
taken to clinging about the place in the form
of the odour of an ill-kept menagerie. Then
there was the company. He had purposely
kept on his rough travelling great-coat lest
the style and completeness of his clothes should
be out of harmony with his surroundings.
Alas! there was no occasion for any such pre-
caution. Of course, he did not expect to see
any of the old faces, or to recognise any that
he might see. But still less did he look to find
himself among a herd of smartly-dressed clerks,

of noisy and probably briefless, but by no
means ill-tailored, barristers, and of a majority
in general which the old *habitués* of the Mare
would have scornfully regarded as snobs and
swells. There were some, it is true, who
might be taken to represent the old press
element which had once been the special glory
of the Old Grey Mare. But even of these the
style seemed to have changed. He had come
to be a silent listener. But where were the
flashes of wit, and the rain of humour, and
the thunders of dispute, that, in his recollec-
tion, had made the place a temple of good
company every day and all night long? Or
was it he, and not the place, that had changed?
Had he once taken chaff for wit, and chatter
for humour? Were these also imagining
themselves geniuses and wits, to wake some
day, like himself, to the discovery that wit
and humour are always things belonging to
one's own youth and no other man's? He
had better have gone to sleep at his club, after
all. Suddenly his eyes fell upon one familiar
object—that of an old man eating a chop, with
a pint of port by his side—the very same old
man who, five-and-twenty years ago, had been
known to eat two chops and to drink a pint of

port at the same hour every day and in the same seat at the Old Grey Mare, who then looked seventy years old, and now did not look more than seventy-one. Surely that old man must be the only reality in a world of shams and dreams.

'An' faith, Esdaile,' said a hoarse brogue in the box immediately behind Sir Charles, 'it was a mighty queer yarn she spun me before she died. "Ronaine," says she—that is to say, "Doctor," says she, "I'd like ye to write a word to me poor father at home—Cox his name is, and so was mine; I was only Stella Fitzjames, ye know, on the boards." "To tell him ye're dead?" asked I. "No," says she, "to tell him I really was a married wife, after all; an' there's my wedding-ring. Tell him if he'll go to Helmforth, to the church there, he'll find the marriage of Mary Cox, that's me, to Rayner Bassett (that was the name) only in another name." "An' what's the name the villain that's left ye married ye in?" says I. "He'll see in the church books," says she. "'Twas Doyle—John Doyle." Now, Esdaile, that was queer. If Rayner had been Charles, we'd have had Charley Bassett and Jack Doyle in the same yarn—a meeting

of the waters, leastway of the names, to make
one think how things are bound to run in pairs.'

'Hum! Things don't run in pairs unless
they're harnessed,' was the answer in the very
tone which had characterised Esdaile the
painter. Sir Charles could almost fancy he
saw the twitch of the corner of the mouth
that used to give an air of irony to his simplest words. 'Nobody ever did know anything of the archdeacon, except that he had
some spite against womankind. I always
thought he must have married, and come to
grief over it in some way. Those big babies
always do. I suppose some Rayner Bassett
has found it convenient to take up with an alias
—that's all. Poor Jack !—or poor Rayner !—
or poor both !—I suppose it's all one, now.
Here's to his memory—Jack Doyle the archdeacon, alias Rayner Bassett the married man !
So that was the end of Stella ! We began
together, she and I ; she played Juliet, and I
painted the balcony. Wouldn't I have roasted
Jack Doyle if I'd only known !'

Surely something more than a chance
impulse must have brought Sir Charles Bassett to the Old Grey Mare. And Esdaile, and
Ronaine, after all these years ! If this were

true, he was no more Sir Charles Bassett than he was that old gentleman who had eaten his chop and drank his port for fifty years, unmoved by the chances—if of chance they be —that make havoc of less philosophic lives.

END OF THE FIRST VOLUME .

PRINTED BY
SPOTTISWOODE AND CO., NEW-STREET SQUARE
LONDON

www.ingramcontent.com/pod-product-compliance
Lightning Source LLC
Chambersburg PA
CBHW060536030726
47498CB00004B/1211